What the critics are saying...

☙

Harm' Hunger

5 Roses! ~ "Ms. Michelle has created complicated characters and strong conflict… As one thing leads to another and the day soon turns into night, and then back into day, an entire love story unfolds, one that will stay with me for a long, long time…" ~ *A Romance Review*

"This first book in the Bad in Boots series is electrifyingly hot, sensual and marvelous. Patrice Michelle writes this tale with strength and knows how to please her readers…" ~ *The Road to Romance*

5 Ribbons! "Patrice has written a wonderfully woven novella, filled with strong sensuality, underlying humor, and above all tenderness! Definitely a hot one! Break out the gloves!" ~ *Romance Junkies*

"The passion Jena and Harm share is explosive…HARM'S HUNGER has it all—tension, drama, romance and great sex! Ms. Michelle did not miss a beat when writing this one. She has earned an instant fan…" ~ *In the Library Reviews*

Ty's Temptation

4 Stars! "Michelle writes a strong, intense tale where the characters and storyline carry a lot of power…" ~ *Romantic Times Magazine*

5 Kisses! "Ty's Temptation is a great western! It's tightly written with characters that leap off the page and right into your heart…Patrice Michelle delivers a fast-paced read you won't be able to put down. It's worthy of the best-seller list!" ~ *RomanceDivas*

5 Hearts! "This is a wonderfully sexy cowboy story. It will satisfy the fantasies of any reader fans of cowboy romances. There is a wonderful eroticism in the love scenes between Evan and Ty…I recommend this book to everyone." ~ *The Romance Studio*

"Patrice Michelle's writing is so expressive I can see and feel what's happening very clearly…Ms. Michelle does cowboys so well. In Ty's Temptation she creates another stunning, hot alpha who makes me want to wrap myself around him and never let go!" ~ *Joyfully Reviewed*

Colt's Choice

RECOMMENDED READ! "Nobody writes sexy cowboys quite like Patrice Michelle…This is one of my favourite books of the year…" ~ *Fallen Angel Reviews*

eCataRomance Reviewers' Choice Award Winner "If I could have given this more than a 5 star rating, I would have. This was such a well-written and well thought out story that it will be hard for any reader to put it down once they start…" ~ *eCataRomance Reviews*

HUNGER AND TEMPTATION

BAD IN BOOTS

PATRICE MICHELLE

ELLORA'S CAVE
ROMANTICA PUBLISHING

An Ellora's Cave Romantica Publication

www.ellorascave.com

Hunger and Temptation

ISBN 1419955357
ALL RIGHTS RESERVED.
Harm's Hunger Copyright © 2003 Patrice Michelle
Ty's Temptation Copyright © 2006 Patrice Michelle
Edited by Sue-Ellen Gower
Cover art by Syneca

Trade paperback Publication Septemeber 2006

Excerpt from *Colt's Choice* Copyright © 2004 Patrice Michelle

With the exception of quotes used in reviews, this book may not be reproduced or used in whole or in part by any means existing without written permission from the publisher, Ellora's Cave Publishing, Inc.® 1056 Home Avenue, Akron OH 44310-3502.

This book is a work of fiction and any resemblance to persons, living or dead, or places, events or locales is purely coincidental. The characters are productions of the authors' imagination and used fictitiously.

Warning:

The following material contains graphic sexual content meant for mature readers. This story has been rated S-ensuous by a minimum of three independent reviewers.

Ellora's Cave Publishing offers three levels of Romantica™ reading entertainment: S (S-ensuous), E (E-rotic), and X (X-treme).

S-ensuous love scenes are explicit and leave nothing to the imagination.

E-rotic love scenes are explicit, leave nothing to the imagination, and are high in volume per the overall word count. In addition, some E-rated titles might contain fantasy material that some readers find objectionable, such as bondage, submission, same sex encounters, forced seductions, and so forth. E-rated titles are the most graphic titles we carry; it is common, for instance, for an author to use words such as "fucking", "cock", "pussy", and such within their work of literature.

X-treme titles differ from E-rated titles only in plot premise and storyline execution. Unlike E-rated titles, stories designated with the letter X tend to contain controversial subject matter not for the faint of heart.

Dear Readers,

I hope you enjoy my Bad in Boots series. I've tried my best to write the books in this series as stand alone titles, but if you'd like a richer reading experience, I recommend the Bad in Boots books be read in the following order…

Hunger and Temptation
Colt's Choice
Hearts Afire (in the *Hearts are Wild* anthology)

All the best,

Patrice Michelle

Contents

Harm's Hunger

~11~

Ty's Temptation

~63~

Also by Patrice Michelle

&

Bad in Boots: Colt's Choice
Cajun Nights *(Anthology)*
Dragon's Heart
Ellora's Cavemen: Tales from the Temple II (A*nthology*)
Hearts Are Wild (A*nthology*)
Kendrians 1 : A Taste for Revenge
Kendrians 2 : A Taste for Passion
Kendrians 3 : A Taste for Control

About the Author

&

Born and raised in the southeast, Patrice has been a fan of romance novels since she was thirteen years old. While she reads many types of books, romance novels will always be her mainstay, saying, "I guess it's the idea of a happy ever after that draws me in."

Patrice welcomes comments from readers. You can find her website and email address on her author bio page at www.ellorascave.com.

HARM'S HUNGER

Dedication

To my first critique partner, Janice Lynn, thanks for encouraging me to keep writing. And thank you for helping me decide on the title for Harm's Hunger.

Trademarks Acknowledgement

The author acknowledges the trademarked status and trademark owners of the following wordmarks mentioned in this work of fiction:

Altoids: Made by Wrigley

Chapter One

ಎ

"What do you mean, you don't know where she is?" Ty Hudson raised his voice and switched his cell phone to his other ear. His dark brows drew together as he rubbed the back of his neck, clearly agitated. "Her flight was due in at three. Did you call her cell phone?" Ty cast Harm an apologetic glance.

Harm placed his booted foot across his knee and leaned back in the seat, sighing. Looked like he might be here a while.

"She probably forgot to turn it back on once her plane landed. Check that she did actually get on the plane and call me back. I appreciate it, Colt." He snapped the phone closed. "Sorry about the delay, Mr. Steele. I know you're anxious to get the papers signed and get back to your ranch, but my sister owns half the property, so I need her signature as well." He ran a hand through his close-cropped hair. "I wish I knew why our great-aunt Sally stipulated we handle the transaction in person if we decided to sell the property."

Harm rose and placed his black Stetson back on his head. "Sally Tanner was a fine woman. I'm sure she had her reasons. I can hang out for a couple more hours." He patted the cell phone clipped to his belt. "You've got my number. Call me when you locate your sister."

As he walked toward the elevators, Harm wondered for the fiftieth time why Sally deeded the land to the Hudsons. They were from the east coast, used to city living, not ranching. Sally had been a great neighbor, letting him use a large portion of her property to rotate his cattle. She'd always claimed, "It's the Texan way, Harmon. You take care of my horses and I let you use the land." And it was as simple as that for Sally. He'd miss the old girl.

As he pushed the button for the lobby, just his luck, the elevator skipped right past the lobby and descended to the basement level. When the elevator doors slid open, two long, shapely legs attached to a very curvy body stepped into the elevator.

Maybe his luck was about to turn.

"Hi." The blonde woman with crystal blue eyes smiled at him as she leaned over to push the button for the eighth floor. She was wearing a barely there, two-piece candy apple red bikini, her hair and skin still wet from the hotel pool she'd obviously taken advantage of. Out of habit, ran his fingers across the brim of his hat. "Ma'am."

She looked him up and down and grinned. "Ooh, a real live cowboy."

"Born and bred." He grinned back.

When the elevator stopped on the lobby floor, Harm was thankful no one was there waiting to get on. He hit the Close Door button, fully intending to bask in this woman's beauty as long as he could. A lift of her eyebrow told him she noticed he didn't punch a button for a different floor. Only the eighth floor button was lit.

As the elevator started to ascend, Harm asked, "Not from around here I take it?" He couldn't place her accent. Virginia maybe? But she had the huskiest voice. It was so damn sexy he wanted to keep talking just to listen to her speak.

She gave a throaty laugh. "No. Just visiting."

As she stared up at the elevator lights, he took a moment to enjoy her luscious curves. Not one ounce of fat graced her nicely built body. She looked to be about five-eight or nine. A nice fit for his six foot three frame. The first stirrings of arousal made itself known in his tightening crotch when he noticed her hard nipples pressed against her wet top. His gaze dropped to her flat stomach and firm thighs. Nice. He'd bet his last dollar she had an ass that begged to be squeezed. But unfortunately she had her hands crossed behind her back, holding a small hand towel against her damp suit.

The elevator stopped on the six floor but the doors didn't open. They both looked at each other and then he punched the button for the eighth floor to get it going again. Nothing happened. He hit the Open Door button but the doors didn't budge.

Harm lifted the emergency handset and dialed the front desk. Once he'd set the receiver back on its cradle, he turned to her and grinned. He couldn't help it. "Well, looks like you're stuck with me for a few."

Now he had a few more minutes with her. It would take the front desk at least fifteen minutes to find maintenance. He put his hands on the guardrail and leaned his back against the sidewall.

She adopted the same position on the opposite wall, laughing. "So sit a spell and all that, huh?"

He chuckled. "Yeah, something like that. Where are you from?"

"Maryland."

"Here for long?"

She shook her head, her eyes twinkling. "Not officially."

A long moment of silence ensued as they both assessed each other. She had a beautiful oval face with almond shaped eyes and eyebrows slightly darker than her hair. But it was her lips that drew his attention. Free of lipstick, her full, naturally rosy lips made him throb. Those lips were made for kissing.

Her unabashed gaze roamed his face and his body while he did the same, this time appreciating the full frontal view. If only he could see her breasts. Were her nipples large quarters or small dimes? He was dying to peel away her bathing su—. Just then, he couldn't believe his eyes, the front snap on her bikini top gave way and her luscious breasts spilled out as the Lycra material snapped backward.

Her sharp, embarrassed intake of breath had him averting his gaze and turning his head, while she faced the wall and made frustrated sounds as she tried to get her suit back together. He tried not to grin. Dimes. Perfect rose-tipped dimes.

"Um, excuse me. Would you mind doing me a favor?" She called over her shoulder?

She's kidding, right? He cleared his throat. "Sure, can I turn around?"

She laughed. "Yes, you'll have to in order to help me."

Harm turned and immediately saw her problem. One of the hooks had caught on the back of her bikini top and she wasn't able to reach it. He had to touch her back in order to release the hook. The brief brush of his fingers against her soft skin only made his cock throb harder.

"Thanks." She let the towel drop so she could fix her top.

Holy shit! What a beautiful ass. He couldn't tear his gaze away from the firm round flesh that the red straps of the g-string bikini framed quite nicely.

She faced him, her eyebrow arched. "Enjoy the view?"

"Hell, yes," he admitted before he thought better of it.

She didn't look angry, just amused. Shrugging, she picked up her towel. "I was trying to avoid that."

His lips quirked upward. "I figured as much." He hadn't moved away and now only a foot separated them. Her scent reminded him of warm sunshine right after a spring rain.

She leaned back against the wall. "You know, I—" Her bathing suit popped open again, exposing her breasts once more. "…am apparently going to keep flashing you," she gritted out, her cheeks turning red as she dropped the towel once more to grab the errant fabric.

"You won't hear any complaints from me. Flash away." He gave his best roguish grin.

"Har-har." She looked up while trying to snap the scraps of material closed.

The elevator started moving and her sarcastic expression turned to panic as they neared her floor. He reached out and pulled the red emergency button to stop the elevator. When he turned back to her she looked about ready to spit nails.

"Can I help?" he offered.

She threw her hands up in frustration, obviously beyond embarrassment at this point. "Have at it."

As he moved closer, she added, "The bikini top, I mean."

He chuckled as he tipped his hat back and picked up the scraps of cloth.

Jena couldn't help but stare at the tall, sexy cowboy as he bent close. The expression on his face was one of concentration as he tried to fix her bikini top. She noted his navy blue button down shirt fit his muscular chest to perfection, showing off his tanned skin.

As he inched closer, his jean-clad leg brushed hers, reminding her of her first reaction to seeing those lean hips surrounded by that faded denim. The material had lighter streaks at the bend of his legs, which drew her gaze to the well-proportioned bulge at his crotch. And now his hot bod was an inch away... *Yum, dee-lish.* She closed her eyes as a frisson of desire coursed through her.

Once she tamped down her raging hormones, she opened her eyes, only to have her gaze zero in on the light brown hair that peeked out beneath his black hat. He wore it a little longer than the super short cuts she was used to. Hmmm, the more to run her fingers through. *Geez, this is ridiculous, Jena. The man's a complete stranger. But, I'm on the extended visual tour. May as well continue.*

Thick brows framed his to-die-for chocolate brown eyes. A straight nose and a strong jaw with a small cleft in his chin finished out his handsome face. Tiny lines appeared around his eyes when he smiled, making him look a little older than the early thirties she guessed him to be.

In all her twenty-nine years, she'd never met a man who smelled as good as this one did. His scent brought to mind the fresh outdoors with a hint of spice mixed in. *Man,* was this tall, sexy, real-life cowboy a hottie. If this was what she'd been missing living in Maryland, she might just reconsider staying in Texas.

She stared at his large hands, tanned from working outdoors. Broad-palmed and long-fingered, he had the sexiest hands she'd ever seen. What would it feel like to have his hard working hands on her?

When his knuckles nudged the plump fullness of her breast, she involuntarily sucked in her breath. Shivers coursed through her body, settling into a throbbing heat between her legs. At her gasp, he stopped his movements and his dark gaze met hers for a long moment, assessing her. He let the cloth drop and smiled while he slowly drew his finger down the inside curve of her breast.

"Ever fantasized about kissing a complete stranger in an elevator?"

Her heart crashed in her chest at his question. God, what a fantasy! *Damn skippy!* Who hadn't had that one?

She tried to smile but couldn't quite manage the expression as revved up as she was. "Yeah, but my fantasy included a tall cowboy wearing a black Stetson."

He grinned and put his hand on the wall above her head. Leaning close, his eyes on her mouth, his lips a breath a way, he said, "I aim to please."

She chuckled at his arrogant stance. "See that you do."

His lips barely brushed against hers as if waiting for an invitation. What'd she have to do, bare her breasts for him? Oh, yeah. She'd already done that. Jena reached up and knocked his hat off so she could run her fingers through his hair. Curving her hand around his neck, she pulled him closer.

When his sensual mouth covered hers, the very first stroke of his hot tongue against hers sent her blood pressure skyrocketing. She moaned into his mouth, and wrapped her arms around his neck as he stepped into her, pressing his very impressive erection against her belly.

He took her mouth with a possessive intensity she hadn't expected. His dominant kiss, as if they'd been lovers for years, was a killer turn on. The tingling sensation scattered all the way through her body and down to her toes.

His hand moved to her naked breast and plucked at her nipple, the rough skin on his fingers a perfect drag against the soft bud. As he kissed her jaw, he grated out, "Just how far does this fantasy of yours go?"

"As far as you're willing to take it." Her chuckle turned to a gasp of pleasure when he wrapped his big hands around her back, pulled her toward him, and closed his mouth over her nipple. Sucking on the hard tip, he rubbed his thumbs on the plump sides of her breasts then gently nipped the pink skin with his teeth.

"Be careful what you ask." His hot breath bathed her breast as he pressed a hand down her belly and slipped it into her bikini bottoms. "I'm a demanding bastard." At his last word, his finger slid past the bikini-cut curls and delved deep into her core.

"Oh God." She inhaled deeply at the delicious sensations engulfing her. "On the demanding thing," she panted, "I think you've met your match."

Chuckling, he kissed a path to her other breast. He sucked long and hard on the hardened tip as he added another finger, strumming her body like the tight cords on a guitar. Jena grabbed his shoulders for support as she arched against his hand.

"How close are you, darlin'?" he asked as he stroked her with masterful purpose.

Her body started to quake and she tensed her muscles around his hand, ready to come. "Very," she gasped.

He withdrew his hand from her body, his fingers sliding her moisture around her clit. "You're so warm and wet. My cock is jealous."

She gritted her teeth when she noted the devilish gleam in his eye. He was toying with her. "Listen, I—"

He shoved his fingers back inside, fast and hard. Her breath hitched and she sighed in pleasure at the rough invasion.

"You were saying?"

"Noth—nothing." Lust engulfed her and moisture rushed between her legs as her entire body bowed, preparing to climax.

"I feel you tightening around me." He leaned close and kissed a path from her neck to her ear where he whispered, "But I want you hotter," and withdrew his hand once more.

"Damn you," she hissed, her body so primed she reached down, ready to finish the job herself.

He grabbed her wrist and yanked her hand away, growling, "Oh, no you don't. You asked for a fantasy. I'm the person who's going to give it to you."

So much blood had flowed south with her arousal—her sex ached and pulsed—he made her hornier than she ever remembered being in her life.

They stood there, glaring at one another

Jena started to pull her wrist away, but he used his hold to tug her against his chest. Before she could push away, he reached for her thighs and lifted, wrapping her legs around his waist as he set her against the wall.

He captured her lips with his at the same time his hands slid up her thighs to grab her ass. His rough hands clutched her close while he drove his erection as far into her as clothes would allow.

She clasped his shoulders and arched against him, tiny whimpers of pleasure escaping her lips.

"You're making a dry fuck feel pretty good," he moaned into her mouth.

Jena laughed, reached between them, and yanked at the buckle on his pants. He backed his hips off just a bit so she could unbutton the top button and slide her hand inside. She took hold of the warm, rigid flesh and touched the tip with her thumb, rubbing the drop of moisture away. She smiled when he groaned and rocked into her hand. As soon as his breathing turned ragged, she released her hold on him.

He lifted his head from kissing her neck and met her gaze, clearly frustrated.

"You need to be hotter," she mocked.

"Damn you."

"Now why does that sound familiar?" Her amusement died a fast death when he pushed two fingers inside her once more, his erection grinding against his hand, adding more pressure. She panted and gyrated her hips as he thrust in and out, rubbing his thumb against her clitoris just as his fingers found her trigger spot deep within.

"Come, sweetheart. Live the fantasy."

Jena dug her fingers into his shoulders. Sensations curled within her, clawing, begging to be released. He shoved his entire body against her, his thick chest, his lean hips holding her up while he stroked her body into a tight coil of raging need.

"Yes, oh God. Yes, *yes!*" She tightened her legs around him, rocking against the rhythmic movement of his hand and grinding hips. He covered her mouth with his, kissing her deeply, taking her breath away as he muffled her scream from her thoroughly satisfying orgasm.

When her spasms finally stopped, he put his forehead on hers and they both continued to breathe heavily.

"We're doing this a little backwards, but…nice to meet you…"

"Jena."

"Jena," he repeated and smiled. "Harm."

She smiled and reached down to stroke his cock. "Now, about your—"

The phone on the wall started to ring, interrupting her but at the same time reminding her they were in an elevator, possibly angering many hotel guests.

Harm withdrew his hand and let her feet slide to the floor as he looked over at the phone. "Rotten timing."

She couldn't help but grin. "At least for one of us."

"Rub it in, why don't you?" He adjusted his pants, retrieved his hat from the floor, and pushed the button back in.

"I still have a problem." She tried to hold her bikini top closed while holding the towel over her bare bottom. She wasn't being very successful. "There are several families on my floor."

He raised an eyebrow. "Hmmm, I see what you mean."

The elevator stopped and sure enough, a family stood outside the elevator waiting for it. Harm reached over, pulled her against his side, and grabbed her butt, towel and all.

"Afternoon, folks," he said in a friendly voice and walked off the elevator with her as if it were perfectly normal for him to have a tight hold on her rear while they walked.

"Um, that wasn't exactly what I had in mind," she said.

"What?" He looked down at her. "You wanted me to shadow you or something?" He shook his head, squeezed her rear, and whispered in her ear. "Uh-uh, darlin'. This is a lot more fun. Your sweet ass was made to be grabbed and often."

Chapter Two

As Jena opened her door, the phone rang. Who would be calling her? No one knew she was here yet. Still holding her bathing suit top together, she walked over to the nightstand near the bed and picked up the phone. "Hello—" She immediately held it away from her ear as her brother lit into her.

"Why the hell didn't you tell me you were coming a day early? I was worried something happened to you."

"There's a reason I didn't tell me. I came to sight-see." She cast a smile toward the cowboy who shut the door behind him, towel in hand.

"Well, it may have taken us six months to finally come to Texas, but I want to get this over with. You've kept Mr. Steele waiting. Get down to my room, 614."

"Now?" She sighed, looking regretfully at Mr. Knock-your-socks-off-with-more-to-come. And boy, did she want to.

"Now."

"Oh, all right. I'll be there in fifteen minutes."

Replacing the receiver, she felt his warm hands settle on her shoulders. Harm gently squeezed and massaged her bare skin. God, he had the magic touch.

"Problem?"

She turned and faced him. "No, but I have some business I need to take care of."

He sighed, disappointment evident in his expression. "Yeah, me too. I'm expecting a phone call." He ran a finger along her jaw, a sexy smile canting the corners of his lips. "How long will you be here?"

His light touch caused goose bumps to form on her skin. "I don't know yet. I may leave as early as tomorrow."

"If this has to be goodbye, I understand." Harm cupped her face in his big hands and brushed her lips with his. He slid his hand through her hair to cup the back of her head and pull her against him. Jena opened her mouth, accepting his intimate, seductive kiss, wanting more.

He lifted his head and kissed the tip of her nose. "I know you have to go." His regretful gaze, heated and intense, dropped to her breasts and then her belly. "The rest of my day won't be near as adventurous."

He touched his hat and turned to leave.

What a gentleman! How many men would just walk away? Jena reached out and wrapped her arms around his waist, dropping her hand to cover the hard outline in his pants, saying in her sexiest voice, "I wouldn't want you to leave empty-handed, Harm, just empty."

Harm stopped dead in his tracks. What a woman! It had been one of the hardest things he had to do—walk away from her luscious body, lust still raging within him. Thank God he wouldn't have to.

She pressed her cheek against his back and slid her hand up and down his arousal. "I do have a few minutes that I could put to some very good use."

Harm gave a low laugh, took his hat off, and threw it in a chair by the table. Jena walked around to face him, slipped out of her bikini top, and unbuttoned his shirt. When his shirt was completely open, she moved to unbuckle his belt and the top button on his jeans. She didn't bother with the rest, just pulled the fabric and the buttons gave way.

Heat curled in his belly, tightening his balls against his body at her aggressive act. Damn, he couldn't remember wanting a woman to go down on him this much. She had lips made for wrapping around his cock, full and firm. If she gave head near as well as she kissed, he'd be in heaven.

Jena pulled back the gaudy green and yellow floral bedspread, pushed him back on the bed, and made fast work of removing the rest of his clothes. When she settled next to him and grabbed hold of his cock, his hips moved involuntarily, bucking into her hand. Before she could touch her lips to him, Harm yanked her across his body, kissing her long and hard. She tasted good, like honey and lemons. He wanted to know what the rest of her tasted like. Too damn bad they didn't have all afternoon to discover each other.

Jena pushed away from him, *tsking*, "As much as I would like to continue kissing your sexy mouth, I have more pressing matters," she tightened her hold on him, "to take care of."

Harm chuckled and let her have free rein. When her mouth closed over him, he closed his eyes and groaned, rocking his hips, pressing further into her hot, wet mouth.

Her tongue slid around the sensitive tip as she sucked and slid her hand down to his balls, playing with him. When she took one of his balls in her mouth, covering it, tasting it with her tongue while she stroked his cock, he almost lost it, but she looked up, tightened her hold and said, "Not yet, Harm."

As she took him fully in her mouth once more, he slid his hand over her bare bottom, squeezed, then cupped her head, changing the pace of her movements, showing her just how he wanted it.

And, fuckin'-A, did she deliver. Jena opened her throat, taking him as far into her mouth as she could, gripping his cock at the base and pumping him, priming him. Oh, God. "Jena," he warned, but she just took more of him further down her throat. Holy shit, he wanted to let go. He had to use his hold on her hair to pull her off him as his body rocked with one of the best damn climaxes he'd had in a very long time.

Jena didn't stop pumping him with her hand until he was completely spent, but she turned angry eyes his way when he was done. "Why the hell did you pull me off you?"

What? Most women would be glad. Harm leaned on his elbow and met her gaze as she got up and threw him the towel. She was obviously pissed.

"Jena, I'm a complete stranger. You don't know anything about my sexual history."

"Is there something you want to tell me?" she shot back.

He shook his head. "No, I'm clean, but I thought it best to not take chances since you didn't know that at the time."

As he got dressed, she appeared to be weighing what he said. "Well, thanks for considering me, I suppose." She sounded disgruntled.

He shook his head, chuckling. "This is the damnedest conversation." He pulled her into his arms. "We certainly don't seem to do things the conventional way, do we?"

She wrapped her arms around his waist and laughed. "Yes, that does appear to be the case."

Harm kissed her temple, "I know you have to go, but will you have dinner with me later?"

She squeezed him and said, "Yes."

He touched his hat and walked toward the door, the hardest thing he'd ever had to do. He didn't want to walk away from her. He paused for the briefest of seconds when he realized he didn't know her last name. Now would be a helluva time to ask. Harm set his jaw. Her last name could be Timbuktu for all he cared. As soon as his business was taken care of, he'd take her to dinner and do his best to convince her to stay longer.

*****

"Mr. Steele is on his way," Ty called out absently as Jena entered his hotel room. Jena's gaze slid to the other person in the room. "Oh, hi, Colt. What are you doing here?" Jena asked her cousin. He sat in a chair against the wall, his cowboy hat resting on his knee.

Colt unfolded his tall frame from the chair, put his hat on his head, and pulled her into a bear hug. "It appears your brother sent me on a wild goose chase for you earlier." He set her back from him and smiled, "Look at you. You're all grown up." His dark brows drew together as a stern expression crossed his handsome face. "But I see you never out grew your fly-by-the-seat-of-your-pants ways, Jena Lee."

Jena sighed. Only the Tanner brothers still called her that. Colt and his two younger brothers, Cade and Mace had teased her mercilessly during the couple of summers she'd spent on her great-aunt Sally's Double D ranch. Their own ranch, The Lonestar, was only a few miles down the road.

"I see you're still ever the responsible one, Colt," Jena teased back.

Colt grinned and touched the rim of his hat, his blue eyes crinkling in the corners. "We all have to be good at something, don't we?"

Ty cleared his throat and settled in a chair at the hotel room desk. He flipped through the paper work and rubbed his square jaw, his vivid green eyes meeting his cousin's across the room. "Colt, thanks for waiting while we settle this." He looked back down at the papers saying, "Why Sally insisted we not use an attorney, but handle this transaction ourselves is beyond me."

Colt settled back in his chair, chuckling. "I think she and her brother were definitely of like minds. The Lonestar's a perfect example."

Ty glanced up from looking at the deed. "Yeah, I couldn't believe it when I heard Uncle James didn't leave his half of the ranch to you, that he left it to his wife, Marie."

Jena noticed the tightening of Colt's mouth before he shrugged and smiled, laughing outright. "Uncle James certainly threw me for a loop. But I've got it all under control. I'm going to buy the land from Marie."

"How do you know she'd sell it to you?" Jena piped in.

Colt grinned. "Marie is retired. She's at a point where she wants to enjoy life, not feel hemmed in by the responsibilities of running a rodeo ranch."

His gaze traveled between Jena and Ty. "Steele is a good man. I see him often at horse auctions. I'm happy to see Sally's land going to him. He deserves it."

Smoothing the short skirt of her yellow linen sundress, Jena settled on the corner of the desk, picked up the paperwork, the deed to the property and house, and smiled. "As for why Aunt Sally asked us to handle the transaction ourselves, I think she wanted us to come back to visit Texas, considering we haven't been here since we were kids."

Her brother snorted while he rolled up the sleeves of his blue cotton dress shirt. "I can do without the heat. I'll take Maryland weather any day."

Jena ran her finger along the desk's smooth surface. "I don't know, I think Texas has a certain appeal."

Ty jerked his gaze to hers. "What do you mean—?"

A knock at the door cut him off. Ty stood up and walked over to the door. Opening it, he extended his hand. "Thanks for your patience, Mr. Steele."

The man walked into the room at the same time Jena looked up. She about had a heart attack. Mr. Steele turned out to be her fantasy cowboy. Heat suffused her face and neck as she watched him shake Colt's hand and mention his latest horse purchase. When he finally met her gaze, his never wavered or showed surprise, though she knew he had to be as shocked as she was.

"I'm sorry about the delay." Ty cut his eyes back to her. "But my sister is a bit of a free spirit at times."

Harm raised his thick eyebrow, and a small smile tilted the corners on his sensual mouth. "You don't say?"

Jena collected her wits and extended her hand, while a secret smile tilted her lips. "Yes, I like to take opportunities as they arise. Jena Hudson. Nice to meet you."

He grasped her hand in a firm grip and met her gaze head on. The blatant look in his eyes told her he approved of her not-so-wet look. "Harmon Steele, Miss Hudson. Pleasure's all mine."

Harm's warm hand made her nipples stand up and rub against her bra, and heat pool between her legs. Jena hoped her brother and cousin didn't notice the flush she knew stained her cheeks. She withdrew her hand from his and took the seat at the desk, needing to put distance between herself and Mr. Too-sexy-for-his-own-good.

"Okay, let's get down to business," Ty said, picking up the paperwork. "Jena, I've already signed my half of Sally's ranch and holdings over to Mr. Steele. We just need your signature."

Harm pulled the check out of his pocket and set it on the desk.

"I'm not signing the deed over."

"What!" All three men said in unison, staring at her with incredulous expressions.

She nodded and sat back in the chair, folding her arms. "I haven't had a chance to visit Sally's place yet. I want to before I make my decision."

"Do you always make it a habit of getting what you want, Miss Hudson?" Harm's Texan accent only accentuated the steely edge in his voice.

She didn't miss his double entendre. The look in his eyes told her he wasn't happy. She jumped up and put her hands on the desk, leaning forward. "No, but I want the decision to be mine, not because people," she looked pointedly at all of the men, "made the decision for me."

Harm crossed his arms over his chest and stared at her, a muscle ticking in his jaw.

Ty coughed. "Um, is there something I'm missing here?"

Jena smoothed a hand over her hair. "No, Ty. I just want to see the ranch, but after the forty-five minute trip from the airport, my rental car died yesterday. Did you get one?"

Her brother pressed his lips together in a thin line. Oh, boy. He was pissed too. Served him right for assuming she'd just sign the ranch away without asking her. Darn autocratic men. All her life men had been making decisions for her. First her dad until his death, then Ty took over with this whole property thing, and now Harm with sex. What's a girl gotta do to show them she has a mind of her own? She grinned inwardly. *Rebel!*

Ty looked at his watch. "No, Colt picked me up and we are meeting Mace and Cade for drinks in an hour."

"I'll take you," Harm said, his voice calm, even.

Jena met his gaze. "I'll rent a car."

"Storm's brewing." Harm jerked his head toward the window. "If you're going to head out to Sally's place, you'll want to beat it."

Jena followed his line of sight. The sky had turned black and menacing, threatening rain. She debated his offer. She really wanted to see Sally's ranch again. It had been fifteen years. And the storm was getting closer by the minute.

"Go on, Jena, let Mr. Steele—"

"Harm."

"…Harm take you to Sally's ranch, get this out of your system, and get back here to sign the papers."

Jena grabbed her purse and eyed all three men. "Fine, but I'm not promising anything."

Harm turned on his heel and walked out. Jena followed, almost running to keep up with him. How did her best fantasy personified turn into her enemy so quickly?

As the elevator descended to the garage, she chanced a glance his way. He stared straight ahead, not once looking at her. That didn't sit well with Jena at all. Thirty minutes ago the man had had his hand down her swimsuit. Not to mention the fact he'd given her the best damn orgasm she'd ever had. And that was with his hand! She could only imagine how the rest of him would feel against her, on her, oh God…in her.

She clamped her legs closed to stop the ache that had started at her wayward thoughts. Somehow she didn't think asking him for a roll in the sack would fly just about now, darn it! But she'd be damned it she'd let him give her the cold shoulder either.

As they entered the garage, she grabbed his arm, pulling him up short. Harm looked purposefully at her hand and then met her gaze with an impassive one.

"Hey, it's not personal, Harm."

He turned to her, his expression angry. "That land should belong to me. I'm offering a fair price for it, and you're standing in my way."

She let go of his arm. "For some reason I can't fathom, Sally left the ranch to Ty and me. The least one of us can do is go see it one last time. Can you understand that?"

He considered her for a moment and then gave a curt nod before he walked toward his red Ford truck. Unlocking her side, he helped her into the cab and shut the door. He walked around to his side and climbed in. Removing his hat and cell phone, he placed them on the seat between them then met her gaze. "It'll take us about thirty minutes to get to Sally's place. I'm hoping we'll beat the storm."

While Harm drove, Jena surreptitiously studied his strong profile. The man was just too good-looking for words. Why in the world wasn't he married? Well, he was already pissed at her. No better time than the present to find out. "So, why aren't you married?"

He gripped the wheel tighter. "That's none of your damned business."

His rough tone didn't intimidate her. "Considering that we've been somewhat intimate, I think that gives me the right."

"That hardly counts."

"Oh, so fly-by-the-elevator encounters are a common occurrence for you?"

He shot her a look. "No, I've never—"

"See, I *am* special." She grinned. "Now give."

Harm set his jaw and stared at the road. For a minute she wondered if he was going to ignore her, but then he finally spoke, "I don't believe in happy-ever-after."

"Whoa, pretty cynical for a man who knows how to fantasize."

Harm cut his eyes over to her, a smartass smirk on his lips. "I didn't say I don't know about pleasure." He shrugged, looking back at the road. "Finding the perfect person to settle down with is a childish fantasy."

Before he had a chance to ask Jena about her single status, rain started falling in heavy sheets. He gripped the steering wheel tighter, concentrating on the road. Lightning slashed across the dark sky, illuminating the road ahead of them. Loud claps of thunder immediately followed. Wind whistled and buffeted the truck, rocking it back and forth.

He cast a glance at Jena as he turned onto the dirt road leading to Sally's ranch. She had a firm hold on the molded door handle, her bottom lip clutched in her teeth.

Damn, it was raining like a sonofabitch. He couldn't see more than two feet ahead of him. Good thing they were almost to Sally's place. Another flash of lightning splintered the sky, and Harm looked up in time to see a huge tree falling right in their path. He slammed on brakes and swerved to avoid the mass of limbs and leaves. The dirt road underneath the tires had turned to slippery muck, allowing no traction when the brakes locked the wheels.

The truck slipped over the side of the road, right into a ditch.

His head slammed into the steering wheel with the force of the impact. Immediate pain followed then blissful blackness.

* * * * *

"Harm? *Harm!*" He heard a woman's frantic voice calling to him, felt her warm hands on his face, his head. Torrential rain pinged on the roof of his truck and thunder rolled in the background, the loud sounds hammering in his aching head.

He opened his eyes and tried to lift his head from the seat. "Sonofabitch," he hissed out as pain lanced through his forehead.

The woman touched his forehead, concern written on her face. "Oh, God, Harm. You were out for about a minute. I was so worried. You're going to have a helluva knot on your head." She held up two fingers. "How many fingers do you see?"

"Two."

She put up two more. "Now how many?"

"Forty." She frowned and he grinned. "Just kidding. Four."

She swatted at his shoulder. "Don't scare me like that. You could have a concussion."

Who was this gorgeous woman? She talked as if she was very familiar with him. Where was she from? Her accent told him she wasn't originally from Texas.

"Uh, well, there is one thing. Who are you?"

Chapter Three

☙

Jena scowled at him. "That's not funny. How can you be joking when we're sitting in a ditch?"

He shook his head, his expression truly puzzled. He reached up and touched a strand of her hair. "I'm not kidding." He tried to smile but winced instead. "Not to say I don't mind sharing close quarters with you and all. Beats sitting in this rainstorm by myself. But I'm drawing a blank, darlin'."

Jena decided to avoid the subject for the time being. If he really did have amnesia, she didn't need to freak him out about that until after they reached Sally's house. If she remembered correctly, her ranch was just up the road.

She held up the broken pieces of his cell phone. "The crash made sure you won't be using this to call for help, but I believe the house is just up the road. Why don't we make a run for it, since the truck doesn't seem to be an option?"

He grabbed her arm before she could unbuckle herself and get out of the cab. "You didn't answer my question."

"How about we talk about it once we're under a roof, okay?" She tried to pull away.

"No. I know we're not far from my neighbor Sally's ranch. Though I'm not sure why we're on this road. I know my name is Harmon Steele and that I'm a rancher. But I'm totally clueless as to how you fit in the picture. I'm not going anywhere until you tell me who you are."

Grrr. If she told him the whole story now, he'd freeze up on her. She wanted to make sure he was okay. No harm in fabricating a little ruse. "I'm Jena." She waited to see if recognition filtered in his expression. Nope. "You know, your girlfriend? You mentioned an errand you needed to run. We were on our way to your neighbor Sally's house."

His brow furrowed. He was tending to Sally's horses, so that made sense. "Why can't I remember you? I think I'd have a hard time forgetting your beautiful face."

Okay, she needed to think about how much deeper a hole she should dig. Avoidance was always a good option. She reached over and opened the door. Gravity pulled the heavy panel out of her hand toward the ditch. "Come on," she said and climbed out of the truck only to ever-so-gracefully crumple to the ground.

Cold, driving rain soaked through her linen dress in two seconds flat. Harm leaned over her seat and poked his head out. "You okay?"

She grimaced and tried to stand and collapsed again, yelping as pain shot up her ankle. Before she could respond to his question, his arms were around her, lifting her against his strong chest.

"Come on, sweetheart, let's get out of this rain."

Sweetheart. That sounded nice coming from his lips. Jena settled her arms around his neck, enjoying the play of muscles surrounding her body, the heat of his skin a wonderful contrast to the cool rain beating on her. Thank goodness he'd put his Stetson back on. The brim provided some shelter from the relentless downpour. She looked up into his face at the same time he looked down at her. God, he took her breath away. The man exuded sheer confidence in every movement he made. He was simply…magnetic.

Harm set her down on the porch, seemingly unaffected by carrying her hundred and twenty pound body the quarter-mile hike up the driveway and across Sally's front lawn. Yep, hard-working man, no doubt, and a considerate one, too, she thought as he handed her the oversized purse she carried around. When he unlocked the door she was surprised to learn he had a key. "You have a key?"

"Yeah. I take care of Sally's horses and such. Now that she's passed on, I keep an eye on her place, too." He lifted her again and walked inside.

When he set her down and stepped away, Jena began to shiver uncontrollably. She set her purse on the table and hugged herself as her teeth began to chatter. "Why is it so cold? Texas isn't supposed to be c-c-c-cold." Her teeth began to chatter.

He met her gaze, his expression completely baffled. "You're my girlfriend, but you don't live in Texas?"

Oh, boy. Now I know where the expression 'snowballing' came from. "Um, well, our relationship is a little complicated."

As lightning lit up the room, he glanced outside and then turned back to her, his white teeth flashing in the darkness. "There's an old saying in Texas—if you don't like the weather, wait around and it'll change."

Harm flipped the light switch. "The storm must've knocked out the power." He lifted the phone receiver. "Phone's dead, too." He walked over to the kitchen cabinets and pulled down a lantern and some matches. Once it was lit, the lantern cast a warm glow throughout Sally's ranch house. Harm carried the lantern and set it down on an end table next to the couch.

Jena looked around as Harm squatted in front of the fireplace to build a fire. The house was just as she remembered it—a stone fireplace, two soft, brown leather couches facing each other, a throw rug woven in earth tones graced the front of the fireplace, a kitchen and dining area melted right into the living room, a bathroom and a bedroom exited to the right. It was a very small, very cozy house.

Harm tossed the cushions off one of the couches and pulled open the foldout bed. As he straightened the white sheets and burgundy insulated covers that were still on it, she asked, "What are you doing?"

He approached her and quickly turned her away from him. As he unzipped her dress, he said, "I'm trying to get us dry and warm."

Jena clung to the material plastered to her skin as he tried to pull it off her body. "Can't we just use towels or something?"

He peeled the sodden dress all the way off. "Nope. Sally requested all her clothes, towels, and sheets be donated to charity when she died. All that's left is what's on this bed and the one in her bedroom." He paused for a second and then continued, "It surprises me that I can remember that, but I can't remember us."

Harm unsnapped her bra, his fingers lingering on her skin before he slipped the straps down her shoulders. "Nice panties," he commented while his hands moved toward her underwear.

Jena kicked off her shoes and slipped her panties off herself. She dove under the covers, grinding her teeth at his chuckle.

Okay, I can handle this. He's just trying to keep me from freezing to death. She snuggled into the warmth of the covers and watched as he pulled the chairs from the kitchen table closer to the fire and hung her clothes over them to dry.

Her breath caught in her throat as he began to peel away his own clothes. Strong, muscular arms surfaced along with broad shoulders and an equally impressive chest. Light brown hair clung to his chest as it veed down to his sculpted abs and narrow hips. Her heart raced as he pulled off his boots and socks then reached for the button on his jeans. As he released the first button, her entire body tensed in suspense. She felt like a voyeur.

Jena looked up and saw his heated gaze on her. He wanted her to watch him. What a turn on! Her mouth went dry at the sight of his long, thick shaft that emerged as he pulled off his wet pants and underwear. He wanted her. She clenched her legs together to put a damper on her swelling lust.

When he turned to put his clothes on the chairs, she appreciated his backside that consisted of two perfectly sculpted balls of muscle. She wanted to cop a feel so bad her palms itched. Jena closed her eyes before she moaned out loud.

A few seconds passed and then the bed dipped as Harm climbed into it. She kept her eyes shut, facing the fire. Maybe he'll...

Jena jumped when he reached over and cupped her breast, using his hold on her to pull her back against his chest. "Mmmm, now this is my idea of getting warm," he purred into her ear before placing a kiss on her neck. "Sit up for a second, sweetheart."

Jena pulled the covers around her naked breasts and sat up, facing the fire. When Harm began to rub her wet hair with a towel, she turned back to him, her eyebrow raised. "I thought you said all the towels were donated."

Harm lifted the kitchen towel. "I remembered these. Your hair is soaking wet. Now turn around so I can dry it."

Jena did as he asked. He'd obviously taken the towel to his own hair because it stood up on his head, going in a zillion crazy directions. How the man look even sexier with his hair tousled, she had no idea, but damn it, he did.

She leaned into his hands and moaned as Harm's long fingers massaged her scalp through the thin towel. The surety of his hands, the warmth of the fire soaking into her skin, made her feel safe and cared for.

When Harm traced a finger down her spine, goose bumps appeared on her arms, making her shiver. "You have a beautiful body, Jena," he whispered as he pulled her down to the bed and rolled her over on her back, bracketing her in with his arms. His handsome face hovered over hers. "Tell me about us." His brow creased. "Starting with your last name. It really bothers me that I can't remember."

She placed her hands on his hard chest, loving the feel of muscles underneath her fingers. "It's Jena Lee." *I'm not really lying. Lee is my middle name.* "We met through a mutual friend and have had kind of a long distance relationship for a little over a year. I live in Maryland. We get together when we can." She chuckled. "That's probably why you can't remember me. I'm not in-your-face every day of your life."

She gulped over the next lie she was about to tell, but she realized now was the perfect time to give Harm his fantasy—the one he seemed determined to refuse to believe in. "You asked me to marry you. I told you I'd come stay for a while and we'd decide from there."

His brown eyes narrowed. "First of all, I'd never settle for a long-distance relationship. Second of all, I'm not a casual sex kind of guy."

She caught herself just before she said, *Shyeah, right. Elevator ring any bells?*

"Third of all, my head hurts from trying to figure out why the hell I'd let you get away in the first place. But it sounds to me like I've been remiss in certain areas or you'd have said yes as soon as I asked."

She chuckled at his arrogant comment. "Pretty sure of yourself aren't you?"

He ran his hand down her cheek and along her jaw line, making her tremble at the feeling of his work roughened hands gently touching her face. "No, I'm sure about us. What I feel when I'm with you is indescribable, Jena."

Her heart contracted at his words. He seemed to truly believe them. She smiled and pulled his head down to hers. "Kiss me, cowboy. And make it a good one."

Harm gently brushed his lips against hers. She melted into him, opening her mouth for a deeper kiss. His tongue caressed hers, mated with her while he cupped her breast in his warm hand.

When he pinched her nipple between his fingers, she arched against him, moaning into his mouth. His thick thigh slid in between her legs as he kissed his way down her jaw and neck before capturing her nipple into his hot, moist mouth.

"Harm," she sighed, pressing closer. "Please tell me you have a condom in your jeans."

His low laugh rumbled against her chest. "Yes, two as a matter of fact, but I want to save them for later." His tongue created a searing path down her stomach as his fingers slipped between her legs. He found her wet slit and immediately plunged two fingers inside.

"*Ohmigod.*" His aggressive invasion put her on the edge of an orgasm.

Harm slowed his pace, saying, "Not yet," as he kissed his way down her navel, pausing to lick the crease where her leg joined her body. She never thought of that spot as an erogenous zone, but he just proved that part of her body was very sensitive indeed. His hot mouth had her juices flowing, gathering for his dining pleasure.

He settled between her legs and laved a hot path from the back of her knee up to her inner thigh, touching her labia, then starting the same path on the other leg. She bucked as he got closer to her wet entrance, but he pressed her hips back down on the bed. "Not yet. I want you wetter."

"I can't get much wetter," she panted.

His dark eyes met hers. "Yes, you can. I want you dripping, Jena. I want more to taste, more to enjoy."

Jena let her head fall back, "Oh lord." His sensual words set an ache coursing through her body. "Touch me, Harm." And he did.

He slid his finger from her clit to that sensitive spot between her vagina and her rectum and pressed. *Holy Jamolie*. She'd never felt anything like that before. Lust surged, hot and heavy, curling through her system. She gripped the sheets and begged. "Taste me."

He dipped his head and swiped his tongue across her slit until he found her clitoris. When he sucked on the responsive bud, she almost bucked him off her.

He chuckled and shoved her hips back down on the bed once more. "You're the damnedest filly I've ever seen. Sit still so I can love you."

"I can't," she gasped when he again slid a finger in her aching, pulsing vagina and pressed on her hot spot deep inside. She lifted her hips once more and begged. "Now! It's too much, Harm, I can't wait."

He tilted her hips and devoured her sex. Jena didn't think she could get any hotter, but the man took her twenty degrees higher. Every stroke of his tongue, every rough rasp had her teetering on the edge of her orgasm.

"God, you taste good. Sweet and musky and..." he groaned against her. "I swear I might come just from the taste of you," he growled and delved his tongue deep inside her slit.

"Don't you dare," she growled back as her hips lifted to meet his tongue's thrusts.

He pressed on her clitoris with his thumb, rubbing the aching nub in small circles. "Come, Jena. I'm hungry. I want *more*."

"Harm!" she screamed as her climax jolted though her, sending vibration after vibration crashing within her. Harm pressed closer, lapping every last drop as if she was the finest dessert and he wanted to lick the bowl clean.

He lowered her hips to the bed, leaned over, grabbed his jeans and pulled, sending the chair over on its side as the soggy pants clung to the furniture. Digging out a condom, he swiftly sheathed his cock and braced himself above her as he settled between her legs.

"Yes." Jena sucked in her breath when the head of his cock slid inside her.

He pushed further into her, groaning as she contracted her sheath around him. Gritting his teeth, he said, "You're so tight. Relax, sweetheart, accept me."

She breathed out slowly, focusing on relaxing and not the stretching of highly sensitized skin.

"Jena, honey, I can't...I have to..."

She lifted her hips and accepted his powerful thrust as he sank to the hilt deep inside her.

He stopped and stared into her eyes. "Are you okay?"

"Yes, I want you deeper," she sighed and rocked her hips.

He bucked at her words, groaning in response as she intentionally clenched her muscles around him.

She put her hands on his shoulders and met his intense gaze. "I want it hard and fast. Don't hold back."

Harm began to move within her, his breathing turning choppy as he withdrew and drove home again and again.

"More," she demanded. And he obliged until the entire couch rocked with their movements. She gyrated her hips and moved her hands to cup his firm buttocks, pulling him closer. "Harder."

"Demanding woman," he ground out as he folded her legs, pressed her thighs to her sides and pistoned into her once, twice more.

He was the perfect length, his cock creating wonderful friction within her. "Harm, oh God, yes!" She screamed as her orgasm hit, flooding through her, rolling into another one as he continued his unrelenting pace until their bodies were spent.

Cupping her face in his hands, he kissed her hard before meeting her gaze with a very determined one. "You're not going back to Maryland."

Before she could reply, he rolled onto his back and pulled her with him, settling her against his chest.

Jena didn't respond to his assumption she'd consent to be his wife. For pity's sake the man had amnesia. He wasn't in his right mind. She ran her hand over the glistening hair on his chest, this time wet from their exertions.

Laying her chin on his chest, she met his languid, melting gaze. "Tell me why you've shied away from marriage until now."

He combed his fingers through her slightly damp hair and gave a half smile. "My parents have stayed in a loveless marriage. I've seen what it has done to both of them. I didn't think I'd ever find someone I'd be willing to spend the rest of my life with. As much as I hate to see my parents unhappy, I respect their commitment to their vows, 'til death do they part. When I marry, it's for life."

"Ah, now I see," she said as she moved to place her head on his chest.

He grasped her chin. "Uh-uh. You're turn. Why did you come to Texas?"

Jena hesitated to answer him. The truth was, not only was she in lust with the amazing man, she really liked him as a person. She'd always trusted her instincts on first impressions. But because of his connection with Sally, she knew more about him. Yeah, he was sexy and adventurous, but his character drew her in the most. He was fair in his business dealings, a great neighbor to Sally, believed deeply in his convictions—a gentleman from his head to his heart. He deserved an honest answer.

"I feel a connection with you on a deeper level." She sighed, flipping her hand. "I know that sounds silly."

"No, it doesn't, Jena. I'd lost faith I'd ever meet someone that felt as connected to me as I do to her." He rubbed his forehead and winced. "How did we meet?"

She looked at his forehead. "You'll have a nasty bruise tomorrow. I believe you have a mild concussion."

He chuckled. "You sound like a doctor."

"Close." She grinned. "Well, kind of. I'm a nurse practitioner." *Oooh, an idea was forming.* "That's how we met. I was here for a medical convention." *Please don't let him ask about the whole 'mutual friend' thing.*

"What mutual friend introduced us?"

D'oh. Damn it, rack your brain, Jena. Think, think, think. What names do you remember Sally saying? Jack. Yeah. Good 'ole Jack.

"Jack."

He drew his brows together. "My foreman? Hey, I remembered something."

Jena smiled in encouragement. "Yeah, he and my dad went way back. My dad told me to stop by and visit him while I was here."

"And that's how we met," he concluded.

"Yep, and the rest, as they say, is history."

"Remind me to give Jack a raise." Harm pulled her closer and kissed the tip of her nose.

She laughed and laid her cheek on his chest. The steady rise and fall with each breath he took, the thudding of his heart, the masculine smell that was all Harm, the feel of the fire, warming her skin. All the sensations lulled her. She was in heaven. If only this were not a fantasy of her own making. If only it were real.

Chapter Four

Jena waited until Harm's breathing leveled off as he fell asleep before she eased off of him and walked over to the window. The storm still raged outside, but with the fire blazing behind her, the house was cozy and warm.

There was just something about Boone, Texas. The picturesque green valleys and crystal-clear streams that filtered off the main river of Sweetwater beckoned to her. But it was more than just the scenery. She couldn't put her finger on it. That pull was the very reason she wanted to see her aunt's place once more before she made her decision.

No matter what happened between Harm and her, she'd made up her mind. She wasn't selling. But what she would do is sell Harm a portion of the land and give Ty his half of the proceeds. That should be a fair arrangement for all concerned.

"What are you thinking about so deeply, darlin'?" Harm asked as he slid his arms around her waist and pulled her back against his hard chest. The deep timber of his voice surrounded her, resonating all the way down her spine. Jena closed her eyes at the feel of his strong arms around her, his masculine scent invading her senses. "I thought you were asleep," she murmured.

He kissed her temple. "I was until I reached over and you weren't there."

He settled her closer against his tall frame. The unmistakable hardness pressing against her bare bottom made hot moisture gather between her legs. God, the man had the most amazing effect on her. She couldn't seem to get enough of him.

"What are you looking for in a husband?"

Jena snuggled into his warmth, crossing her arms and laying them over Harm's. "Someone who will let me make my own decisions, who will respect my need to do so, even if he disagrees with my decision."

Harm placed a featherlight kiss on her neck. "What if there are times when your husband does know best?"

Jena stiffened in his arms. Harm tightened his hold, not letting her pull away as she intended. "Then he'll learn real fast, I make up my own mind."

"What if he's just as stubborn as you?" He slid his hand up her waist and cupped her breast, then twirled the nipple.

Jena sucked in her breath at the achy desire his touch roused within her. "Then we'll have problems," she breathed out, breathless, trying to keep a firm hold of rational thoughts.

Harm slid a hand down her abdomen, spearing his fingers through her curls until he reached her labia. He drew his finger along her clit in a slow, lingering rub. "What if he's willing to compromise?"

Jena bucked against his hand. Her breathing turned shallow as she lifted her arms and wrapped them around Harm's neck. Thinking became very difficult as he circled his finger around her sensitized bud. "Com-compromise?"

"Pick a number. One." He slid a finger inside her and she groaned. "No, two." He added another finger, creating pressure with the sensuous glide of his fingers, wet from her juices, rubbing in and out of her sheath. "Ah, I think three is the lucky number." When a third finger joined the other two, he cupped her mound with his hand and drew her up and back against him, holding her still, no longer moving his hand.

"Three times a year, your husband gets carte blanche on a unilateral decision that concerns you. He may or may not exercise his rights, depending on whether the situation warrants it. What do you say?"

He touched her clit with his thumb and made a small circle against her flesh. Jena whimpered and rocked her hips, wanting to move, needing the release her body sought. "Only if I get three for him as well."

Harm's chuckle rumbled against her back. "Quite the negotiator, aren't you?"

"Yes," she said impatiently, "and right now I'm ordering you to give me what I want."

"No, Jena, I'm going to give you what you *need*." He kissed the sensitive place behind her ear. "Me," he said in a husky tone as he moved his fingers in and out of her body, his thumb applying steady pressure against her clit. At the same time, his other hand slid to her breast and clasped the plump flesh in a possessive hold.

"Harm, oh, God, that feels so good," she panted and rocked into his hand.

While his hand continued to thrust against her sex, Harm slid his fingers to her nipple and swirled the hard bud. His actions sent Jena over the edge. Her body trembled with the force of her orgasm. She cried out at the pure pleasure spiraling from her sex and breasts to her stomach and thighs and beyond.

Once her heart rate slowed, she turned, only to have it speed right back up. She stared in fascination as Harm's gaze locked with hers while sucked her cum off each finger, one-by-one, groaning his approval. Pure lust in its most primal form slammed in her stomach as she watched him savor her taste.

After he finished, his eyes were so dark brown, they almost looked black. When he started to speak, her stomach made a gurgling sound. Jena laughed in embarrassment.

Harm glanced down at her stomach, an apologetic look on his face, "Are you hungry? All I have to offer you are apples and carrots." He gave her a lopsided grin. "Horses love 'em as a treat."

She returned his smile with a knowing grin. "Yes, I'm hungry." Reaching out, she wrapped her fingers around his rigid cock and ran her thumb over the drop of pre cum that moistened the tip. "But I'm in the mood for protein, not fruits or vegetables."

Harm eyes blazed with naked desire. His gaze dropped to her lips, and his nostrils flared as a small smile quirked the corners of his lips. "Never say I don't know how to provide the most important food group for my woman."

His woman. That sounded just right to her. Jena pointed to the kitchen chair in front of the fireplace. "Go sit."

Harm grinned and followed her orders. He heard her rummaging around in her purse while he moved some wet clothes to another chair. Positioning the empty chair in front of the fire, he sat, waiting for Jena.

Jena. She was the most stimulating woman. Why in the world had he let their explosive relationship go on for a year before he decided to do something about it? Thank God he came to his senses. His stomach tightened into knots when he realized his own stubborn convictions could have pushed this wonderful woman into another man's arms. Harm clenched his jaw in anger at the mere thought. She was his. Period. Never before had he felt so strongly about another person. The realization his feelings went so deep threw him off-balance.

Jena's hand brushing over his shoulder drew him out of his reverie. Harm reached up to clasp her around the waist, intending to bury his face in her breasts. "Uh-uh." She pulled away and stood facing him. "No touching."

Harm raised an eyebrow. "Is that the way it's going to be?"

She smiled and nodded. Tapping her finger against her lips she took a slow circle around the chair, eyeing him up and down. Desire and mischief filled her gaze. She appeared to be deciding just what she wanted to do with him. Harm's cock throbbed against his belly in anticipation.

She stopped in front of him once more and laid her hands on his thighs. When she slid them to the crease in his legs and touched his balls lightly with her thumbs, he shuddered. She jerked his thighs further apart, and Harm groaned at the lightning lust that surged through his body at the mere thought of what she had planned. He lifted his hands to cup her breasts but she backed away, shaking her head.

Now he understood. If he touched her at all, she'd stop. Harm clenched his jaw and clamped his hands on the bottom of the chair. Damn, it was the only way he'd keep from touching her. She was a gorgeous sight to behold. The fire reflected off her peach-toned skin and honey-blonde hair, making him ache to touch her just to see her cheeks flush with desire once more. Perfect breasts, more than a handful, and ruby red nipples, jutted out impudently at him, teasing him, torturing him. He wanted to taste her so bad, his mouth watered.

When she went down on her knees in front of him, Harm held back the growl of satisfaction that threatened to rip from his chest. Jena traced the inside of his thigh with her tongue until she reached his balls. His throat tightened when she flicked the bulging veins with the tip of her tongue. Harm's hips moved of their own accord, closer to her hot mouth. But she moved to his other leg and repeated the same process all over again until her mouth rested over him. She gave him a minx-like smile as she grasped his cock with one hand and fondled his balls with the other.

"Taste me, Jena." The request was out before he could stop himself.

She tortured him with her tongue once more, touching every ridge and vein in his cock as she licked a path along the entire length of his erection. Harm's balls tightened in erotic anticipation, and his stomach tensed as he waited for her mouth to surround him. His fingers itched to brush against the curve of her spine, to connect with her soft skin, but he tamped down the urge. Later, he promised himself.

When she closed her mouth over him and stroked his erection with her tongue, the unexpected cool, tingling sensation nearly rocked his world. Harm took deep breaths to keep from losing it so quickly. As she worked her mouth up and down his length, he managed to rasp out between building, coiling tension and ragged breaths, "What do you have in your mouth? It feels incredible."

"Hmmm," she hummed her response and he bucked against her as the vibrating sensation spread like wildfire throughout his lower torso and thighs.

Harm gave in to his natural inclination. Without thinking, he placed a hand on the crown of her head and directed her to take him further down her throat. Jena's eager accommodation to his silent request had him groaning his approval. Her sensual nature shook him to the very core, sending an odd sense of déjà vu rocketing through him and making oral sex with Jena that much more exciting.

He lifted his hips and rocked against her hot, moist mouth, hissing out, "Jena," as she took a long, sucking drag on his cock. When she bit down then circled his shaft with her tongue as if soothing her love nip, pleasure-pain shot through him, taking him to the brink of his orgasm. He held back, wanting to prolong the thousand jolts of awareness that centered with her mouth on his cock and radiated throughout his body.

He caught the scent of her own arousal and heard her moan, and Harm was lost. He groaned and let go, rocking hard against her warm mouth as he came. The knowledge that Jena took everything he offered with pleasure made his orgasm one of the longest, most fulfilling climaxes he'd ever experienced.

Once she'd licked him clean, Jena stood and placed her hands on his shoulders. The scent of peppermint surrounded him as she leaned over and said, "Altoids," before she kissed him deeply. He lifted his hands to pull her into his lap, but she drew back with a wicked grin.

"You see, the reason I would even consider agreeing to your compromise is because I know who *really* wields all the power."

"Oh, you do, do you?" Harm gave her a devilish smile and before she could move away, he swiped his finger along her slit, gathering the sweet cream he knew awaited his touch. While she gasped her surprise at his knowledge of her arousal, he raised a cocky eyebrow and slid the wet finger into his mouth, sucking her juice away.

He pulled Jena between his legs and captured her lips, his kiss possessive and thorough. She sighed against his mouth, melting into his body. His heart skipped a beat with the knowledge that he loved his woman so much it scared him. Those three chances were as much for his sanity as hers. Otherwise, she would have him completely wrapped around her finger even more than he already was. He vowed to himself before the evening was out, he'd have Jena as addicted to him as he was to her.

* * * * *

Harm set her on the floor and pulled the chairs out of the way. "Wait here. I'll get us some food."

Jena watched the flex and play of his taut butt cheeks as he walked toward the kitchen. The display of muscles and naked male flesh made her weak in the knees. She couldn't believe how well they'd connected. What would he say when his memory came back? Would he despise her? Her stomach pitched at the thought.

She shook her worried thoughts away. She didn't want to think about it tonight. If Harm didn't get his memory back by tomorrow, she'd tell him the truth. A crackle and hissing pop from the fire drew her attention. The heat felt so good against her skin. She touched her clothes and sighed at the still damp material. Deciding to bask in the fire's warmth, she lay down on the rug and stretched out on her belly, waiting for Harm.

The smell of apples invaded her senses. Jena lifted her head from her cradled arms. She smiled at Harm as he drew the apple slice away from her nose and popped it into his mouth. He'd apparently turned out the lantern, and the surrounding darkness made the glow of the firelight feel that much more intimate.

"Hey, sleepyhead." Harm leaned back against the foldout bed and propped his elbow on his bent knee, totally at home with his nakedness in front of her.

Why did it seem perfectly natural to be lying there naked in front of him? Jena stretched and smiled. "Guess the fire put me right to sleep."

"Yeah, didn't have anything to do with your earlier exertions, I'm sure," he teased, winking at her.

Damn, he was one sexy man. Jena chuckled and rose up on her elbows to take a slice of apple off the plate he'd set between them. "Oh, I suppose it might have something to do with that, too." She nibbled on the piece of fruit. "So, your turn. Tell me what you're looking for in a wife."

He shifted his gaze to the fire. "I want someone who accepts what I am—a rancher, no more, no less—who is willing to live that lifestyle with me. Someone who attracts me both mentally and physically." His eyes met hers. "Someone that I can enjoy the give and take of debating with just as much as the give and take while making love and…" Heat curled within her belly as Harm paused to rake his gaze across her naked back and buttocks. His dark eyes met hers as he continued, "I've found her."

Jena swallowed the piece of apple that threatened to lodge in her throat. She rolled onto her side, propped up on her elbow and faced him. "Harm, all I said was that I would come and stay for a while."

Her heart raced as Harm pushed her on her back and leaned over her, his hands braced on the floor around her. "I thought I said this already. You're not going back to Maryland, Jena." He punctuated his words while kissing a path along her throat.

She pushed at his shoulders until Harm lifted his head. "And I told you I make my own decisions."

His chuckle was low, but his expression serious. "Didn't I tell you? I'm exercising my right at a unilateral decision on your behalf. In this case, I definitely know what's best for you."

Jena laughed at his self-assured confidence. "But that was as my husband."

He raised an eyebrow. "As far as I'm concerned, I'm already your husband. And as you know, I don't commit lightly."

"All the more reason for you to really think before you commit yourself." *Okay, I'm really feeling like a heel now. He's going to kill me when he gets his memory back. At the very least, he'll never forgive me.* Jena pushed at his arms, needing space. Harm leaned back and let her rise, the look on his face inscrutable. She couldn't fathom what he was thinking.

Without a word, he stood and lifted her in his arms. Setting her on the bed, he climbed in behind her then pulled her hips back until her butt rested against the cradle of his hips and thighs. As he settled his chest against her back and rested his hand possessively on her hip, Jena wished he'd never bumped his head, that she hadn't set this whole fabricated fantasy in motion. But then if she hadn't, maybe Harm would've treated her differently, continued to hold a part of himself back, and she would never have gotten to know the real Harmon Steele.

* * * * *

"Don't move," Harm whispered in her ear. Jena surfaced from her deep slumber when he laid his body, hot and naked, across her back. He laced his fingers with hers and silently directed her to curl her hands around the mattress edge above her head.

Her skin prickled in sexual excitement as he slid his palms down her back to the indention of her waist. The fire had died to dull red embers and the sound of rolling thunder sounded far off. Only an occasional flash of lightning illuminated the otherwise pitch-dark room.

Jena sucked in her breath when he lifted her hips. She started to rise up on her hands and knees, but Harm put a hand on her back, forcing her to remain as she was—her butt tilted in the air, her face on the pillow, arms stretched above her, clutching the bed.

When he slid a finger inside her and slowly turned it around, finding and pressing on her g-spot, she bucked against his hand. His touch disappeared and she started to sit up and complain, but the sensation of his thumbs spreading her sex and his mouth sucking her clit had her collapsing with a sigh of pleasure.

"I can't get enough of you." Harm alternatively tugged her clit and laved her juices that gathered in response to his expert manipulation.

Jena had never felt so decadent and excited in her life. She clutched the foldout mattress and rocked against him, raging need building inside her.

"The give and take, Jena, remember," he murmured against her body as he worked his fingers inside her vagina long enough to make her juices flow and then traced every crevice of her sex with his tongue, lingering, leisurely enjoying what her body naturally provided before he'd start the same process over again and again.

Her thighs trembled and her body quaked with need. He was driving her insane. Only the occasional thrust of his tongue deep within her heated core or flicking against her aching nub marginally assuaged her building desire. Damn, he was skilled at oral sex. She'd never met a man who seemed to get off on tasting her as much as Harm did.

He slid a finger in her sheath once more while he planted a kiss on the curve of her rear end and said in a serious tone, "Do you trust me, Jena?"

Jena was about out of her mind, her body demanding release from the sinfully tortuous path he'd lead her down. "Yes," she managed to say between pants. In her heart, she knew she did. Her pulse raced as she waited for Harm's response.

Harm pushed her thighs further apart and slipped something — what was that? A piece of ice? — inside her. "Ohmigod," she cried out and rose up on her hands and knees as her entire core suddenly went from raging hot to freezing cold.

Cupping his hand over her entrance, Harm held her body closed while he slid his fingers back and forth against her clit. With one hand continuing to work against her sex, he laid his chest over her back and used his other hand to tweak her nipple. His lips landed on her shoulder in a tender kiss.

"Come for me, Jena. Let that tight, warm, sweet-tasting pussy of yours melt the ice the way you melt me."

The cold no longer existed. Only the hot, husky need in his voice and the pent-up tension within her remained. Jena moved with the motion of his hand, seeking fulfillment. She whimpered and rocked at the clawing need raging within her. But it wasn't until Harm pulled back and swiped his tongue in a long, reverent lick against her clit, that she felt the first tremors of her orgasm take over. She moaned and tightened her body, preparing herself.

Before she could come, Harm immediately sat back on the bed and pulled her back against his chest. He groaned as he slid his cock inside her, lowering her hips over his thighs. Back to chest, soft thighs surrounding his rock-hard ones, Jena gasped in sheer delight. Her muscles flexed as she lifted herself up and down his rock-hard cock, enjoying the full feeling within her sensitized sheath.

Harm rolled her clit between his fingers and rasped as his breathing turned labored, "The next time we make love I'm not wearing a damn condom."

Jena sobbed as her body shuddered with the most powerful orgasm she'd ever experienced. Harm had ruined her for all men but him, for she knew without a doubt she was hopelessly addicted to Harm's hunger.

Chapter Five

ഇ

Harm awoke the next morning feeling stiff all over yet mentally rested. His head throbbed but it didn't compare to the jerking of his heart when he saw Jena wasn't in bed. Her clothes were gone from the chairs as well. As he quickly dressed in his jeans, the phone rang. He dove for it, jamming his toe on the kitchen cabinet in the process.

"Hello?" he growled in anger at the pain radiating from his foot.

"Harm?"

"Yeah?" He racked his brain, but the male voice on the other end of the line didn't sound familiar at all.

"Ty here. I've been trying to reach you all night. Man, that was a hell of a storm last night. I'm assuming you and Jena stayed at Sally's place to ride it out. Did she make up her mind to sign the papers yet?"

Hell of a storm.

Sally's place.

Sign the papers.

The phrases triggered Harm's memories, and they all came flooding back—Jena and he and the elevator. Jena refusing to sign her half of the ranch over to him. The trip to Sally's place. The storm. The wreck.

"Harm? You there?"

"No, not yet, but I'm working on it. We'll give you a call back in an hour."

As he hung up the phone, Harm felt like he'd been sucker-punched in the gut. Anger, his first reaction, was quickly replaced by fear. The idea that all they'd shared last night was nothing more than a fantasy, made him feel sick to his stomach. His thoughts swirled as they shifted to Jena and her motivations. Why did she create an entire relationship where one didn't exist? One thing he knew for certain. His feelings for her were very real. Did Jena feel the same or were the things she said last night an act, too?

Noticing her purse still on the table, he assumed she wouldn't leave it behind. Harm didn't bother buttoning his pants the rest of the way. To hell with his shirt. He had to find her.

Fortunately, he didn't have to look far. She stood next to the fence rubbing Flash's neck and mane. Against the outline of the rolling pastures, Jena and her fitted yellow dress made a beautiful picture. Milky skin, the Texas sun shining down on her blonde hair as the wind blew the silky tendrils around her shoulders.

As he approached, he heard her crooning to Sally's favorite mare. He'd yet to move the horses. He wanted to own the property outright before he made decisions about them.

* * * * *

Jena jumped when Harm's hands landed on her hips, pulling her into his arms. She snuggled close, enjoying the warmth of his strong embrace surrounding her, his naked chest touching her bare shoulders.

"How's your ankle?" he asked.

"Much better." She laid her head against his neck. "Sleep well?"

"Yeah, except for being shaken awake every hour, only to be told to go back to sleep."

Laughter bubbled up at his disgruntled tone. "It was for your own good. You had a mild concussion. I wanted to make sure you were okay."

He kissed her temple. "Do you know you have the sexiest voice? It makes me hard as a rock in record time."

"And here I thought other parts of my body did that to you."

His hands covered her breasts and his thumbs brushed across her nipples through the linen material of her dress until they pebbled into hard nubs. "Wouldn't want these babies to feel neglected, darlin'." Jena sighed as he slid the straps of her dress down, exposing her breasts to the open air.

When he rolled her sensitized nipples between his fingers, she moaned at his touch, arching back against his hard erection. He groaned and said as he nuzzled her neck, "Remember what I said last night about the next time we made love?" He slid his hands down her thighs. "I want to feel the moisture of your hot, wet skin sliding against my cock, Jena. I don't want anything between us anymore."

She stiffened in his arms, guilt assailing her at her deception. Was it wrong when it felt so right with Harm? She was on the pill, so the only chance she'd be taking was between them and their future relationship. When he regained his memory, she hoped he forgave her. His hands clasped her hips, pulling her tighter, seeking a response.

"Yes, I remember." She pushed back against him, giving him his answer.

Her heart raced, her stomach clenching in excited anticipation as she felt him unbuttoning his pants behind her. Liquid heat pooled between her legs when he lifted the fabric of her dress upward, revealing her behind.

"What a sweet ass." He cupped her bare flesh and squeezed. "This g-string is a definite turn on."

She gasped when he traced his finger down the strap between her cheeks until he reached her wet center. "I'm glad you approve," she said breathlessly.

He kissed her shoulder as he slipped his finger inside her. "Thongs will be a requirement for the next fifty years or so. But for now," he pulled her panties down her hips, "I don't want anything in my way."

As Jena stepped out of her underwear, the fierceness of his tone struck a cord within her. She covered his hand on her breast with hers, stilling his movements. She couldn't continue deceiving him this way. He believed they were at a different point in their relationship and he deserved the truth. She started to turn, to tell him the truth, but he clasped his hand firmly on her breast and held her in place as he slid his cock inside her.

Sheathed to the hilt, he whispered in her ear, "I want a wife. I want two or three or a passel of kids. I want it all and I want it with you." He withdrew and sank back home once more, causing her breath to hitch in her throat as she grasped the fence for support.

"You never did officially answer the question, so I'll ask you again." His broad-palmed grip on her hips tightened. "I've fallen in love with you, Jena Hudson. Will you marry me?"

The emotions warring within her—guilt, desire, lust, love—they all hiccupped when she realized he'd said her real name.

She looked at him over her shoulder and whispered, shock making her voice quiver, "When did you get your memory back?"

He regarded her with his dark, probing gaze. "This morning when your brother called to check on us."

"Oh, God." She turned away from him, tears stinging in her eyes. "I'm sorry, Harm. I just wanted to give you your fantasy. I hope you can forgive me."

He clasped her breasts and pulled her back against his chest. "Only if you'll say yes, Jena. You have the power to make my fantasy a reality. It's your decision."

His words warmed her heart. She let the tears fall. "Yes, Harm. Yes, I'll marry you."

"Thank God." He expelled a breath.

She gave a watery laugh at his obvious relief.

"And by the way, don't expect me to ever wear a condom again. I don't care how many kids we have. This feels too damn good to ever go back."

Jena placed her hands on the fence again and shamelessly pushed against him. "Then finish what you started, cowboy."

"Happy to oblige, ma'am." He chuckled and grasped her hips once more as he pulled out and plunged in, deep and hard.

Each thrust took him deeper as if he was making love to her for the first time...and in a way, he was. The mere thought made Jena's heart skip several beats. She arched her back and contracted her muscles, smiling when he groaned at her actions. Her smile faltered and she gasped when he slid his hand down her hip, across her lower belly and found her swollen clitoris, rolling it between his fingers.

"I love you, more than I could imagine possible," he said, his voice taut with need. "Come for me, sweetheart, the first of many for the rest of our lives."

And she did, more than once as he rammed into her, the sensations engulfing her. Her climax splintered in tingling waves through her body, the sheer intensity making her shake all over.

Harm pulled out of her and immediately turned her around. Wrapping his hands around her waist, he lifted her up in the air and settled her against his cock. As he kissed her, he slid her sex down around his erection, slick with her juices.

"Mmmm, not one damn thing compares to this rubbing of flesh against hot, wet flesh," he groaned out. Cupping her bare buttocks to protect her skin, he leaned against the fence, withdrew and thrust back in, hard and deep. Jena keened her pleasure over his aggressive coupling. She clasped her legs firmly around Harm's waist and gyrated her hips, clenching her muscles around him, wanting him aching with need.

"Jena," he said in a husky voice as she felt his body tense.

She rocked against him once more to send him into orgasm, but he held on, thrusting and pressing against her until her own orgasm started. "Yes, Harm, *yes!*" she screamed. She rode his hard pace until they both climaxed.

Harm set her on the ground and silently pulled her back against his chest, wrapping his arms tight around her. She laid her head against his shoulder and watched the horses running in the lush, greed pasture. "Um, you do know you only have two chances left, right?"

As Harm's chest rumbled with laughter, Jena smiled and whispered, "Thank you, great-aunt Sally."

* * * * *

"What do you mean 'I have to stay on a little longer'? I need to get back to Maryland, Jena." Ty looked about ready to explode as he paced in his hotel room.

Jena reached over and clasped his shoulders, kissing her brother on the cheek. "I need you to give me away at the wedding, silly. And of course, we'll fly Mom here."

Ty's shocked gaze darted back and forth between them. Harm had to fight the chuckle that threatened to his escape his lips. He kept his expression perfectly composed as he handed Ty a check for his half of Sally's property. "Looks like we're going to be brothers, Ty." Harm clasped him on the shoulder as a big Texan grin rode his face. "Welcome to Texas. Stay a while and you'll never want to leave."

"Heaven help me." Ty groaned and rolled his eyes.

Jena waggled her eyebrows. "Oh, I don't know, Ty. Never say never. Texans have a way of growing on you."

Harm pulled her into his arms and kissed the tip of her nose. "That we do, darlin'. That we do."

TY'S TEMPTATION

Dedication

I wanted to give a huge thank you to my critique partner Cheyenne McCray and my editor Sue-Ellen Gower for their help on Ty's Temptation!

Trademarks Acknowledgement

The author acknowledges the trademarked status and trademark owners of the following wordmarks mentioned in this work of fiction:

Altoids: Made by Wrigley

Coke: The Coca-Cola Company

Mustang: Ford Motor Company

Chapter One

"Is that your red 'Stang out in the parking lot?"

Ty finished paying for his soda and turned to the blond teenage boy who'd tapped him on the shoulder. "What?"

The kid jerked his head toward the gas station parking lot. "The Mustang? Is that your car?"

Ty nodded and gave the kid an indulgent smile while he unscrewed the cap on his Coke. He took a long swig and enjoyed the brief relief the cool beverage provided from the fall Texas heat.

"Aaaaah," he let out a sigh of satisfaction as he twisted the lid back on. "It's a rental, but it's my car while I'm visiting."

The boy smirked at the sound of squealing tires. "Looks like it's someone else's car now."

Ty jerked his gaze to the parking lot in time to see the taillights of his rented sports car shoot into traffic. His heart raced and anger quickly slammed to the surface. He faced the boy once more.

"Why didn't you say something sooner?"

The kid put his candy bar on the counter so the clerk could ring it up and shrugged. "Hey, I just saw him get into your convertible. I didn't know if the guy was with you or not."

Ty took a calming breath and jangled his keys in front of the kid. "Seeing him hotwire my car didn't clue you in?"

The teenager handed his money to the young female cashier who seemed to be listening to their conversation with interest. He peeled away the wrapper and then took a bite out of his candy bar. The strong smell of peanuts and chocolate drifted

Ty's way as the boy tilted his head and spoke with his mouth full.

"Maybe you shouldna' left your top down."

* * * * *

Ty drove along the tree-lined dirt road that led to his great-aunt Sally's Double D ranch. Gravel crunched under his tires as he rolled to a halt in the driveway in front of the small one-story house. He opened the door, climbed out of the cramped, two-seater sports car and grimaced as he pressed the palm of his hand against his stiff spine. *That'll teach me to ask for the first available convertible.* Ty pulled his cell phone from his pocket and leaned on the car's hood as he dialed Jena's cell.

"Hello."

"Heya, Sis, I'm at the Double D. Thanks for sending me the key."

"Ty! Where have you been? I tried your cell but you must've had it turned off. I expected you to come by Steele Way and have lunch with us hours ago. You've made me hold off the wedding for a couple of months now while you finished your project. I want you to see Harm's ranch, and spend some time getting to know my fiancé."

"That 'project' was a twenty-million-dollar, state-of-the-art building, Jena. It did wonders for Hudson & Shannon's reputation in the architectural community." He rubbed the back of his neck and felt the weight of the four-hour police interview and annoying paperwork with the car rental agency finally start to take its toll.

"I'll see you tomorrow, bright and early. Let's just say I've had a heck of a day. I want to hit the hay early tonight."

"Is everything all right?" she asked, concern in her voice.

He ran a hand through his hair and down the five o'clock shadow on his jaw, chuckling. "Yeah, but I don't think the Hudsons have the best of luck with rental cars."

"Oh no! Did your car die on you, too?"

"Worse. It was stolen."

"You're kidding me!"

Ty gave a tired sigh. "I wish I were."

"I'm so sorry that happened."

He shrugged. "It's not a problem. I'll see you tomorrow."

Ty closed the phone and opened the car door to pull out his suitcase. The empty backseat reminded him his stuff was still in the stolen car. Thinking of his expensive clothes packed in that suitcase, he grumbled as he headed for the front door, "I hope he's too short for my clothes."

As soon as he unlocked the door and walked inside, Ty noticed two things—Jena kept her promise to have the place ready for him, and he couldn't get enough of the smell permeating the room. Cinnamon and apples.

He glanced to the left of the entryway to the kitchen and grinned when he saw a pie sitting on the stove. Jena knew how much he loved apple pie. His gaze continued around the small house. The kitchen flowed right into the living room where a couch and rug sat in front of the fireplace hearth. A big picture window took up the wall straight ahead of him and two doors lined the wall to his right. The door farthest away led to the only bedroom. The door next to it led to a two-way bathroom that also opened into the bedroom.

His gaze circled back around to the small, efficient kitchen with its wooden table and four chairs. The place looked exactly as he remembered it. Small and cozy. He smiled in memory of Jena's and his past summer visits with his great-aunt Sally, even if he did spend his summer nights sleeping on a foldout cot so Jena could have the sofa bed.

"I miss your spunky self, Aunt Sal." He regretted he didn't get a chance to see her one last time before she passed away.

You'd better wash those hands and freshen up before you dare to sit at my table. Her voice entered his head as if it were yesterday and not eighteen years since he'd last seen his aunt.

He headed toward the bathroom, and as he walked past the end table next to the couch he noticed the paring knife and plate his sister had obviously forgotten to take back to the kitchen. Shaking his head, he chuckled at the fact some things never changed. Growing up, Jena had always forgotten to put her dishes away.

Ty started to put his hand on the bathroom's doorknob when the door jerked open. A tall woman wearing nothing but a fluffy white towel around her body started to walk out of the bathroom.

"Aaaaahh!" she screamed, taking a step back.

Ty raised his hands in innocence at the shocked look on her face. "Hey, I—"

Before he had a chance to finish, she'd removed her oversized towel and threw the cloth over his head, blocking his view.

His heart raced at the strange scenario, but hey, he was a man. Ty reached up to grab the towel from his face in hopes of catching a glimpse of her naked body. A jolting blow to the back of his knees caused his legs to buckle. Another hit behind his ankles sent his feet flying out from underneath him. He landed flat on his back and air whooshed out of his lungs from the sudden impact. *What the hell?* Still reeling and trying to catch his breath, Ty heard a loud crash on the wooden floor next to him. His heart raced and he tried once more to remove the towel. But instead of finding freedom, his wrists were quickly bound, followed by his ankles.

When the towel flew off his face, he tried to sit up. Ty noted the broken dark blue ceramic shards on the floor as he struggled against the electrical cord wrapped around him.

The woman leaned over him. One hand clutched the towel to her breasts and the other held a paring knife pointed at him. "Move even one inch and you'll find out the hard way I'm not afraid to stick you like the trussed-up pig you are." She straightened and backed away, her movements slow and cautious.

Water dripped from her hair onto the delicate slope of her shoulders, disappearing in the valley between her breasts. Now that she'd stopped moving, he realized her hair was a light color. Blonde maybe?

Obviously he'd scared the shit out of this woman. Despite the misunderstanding, Ty couldn't help but be impressed by her quick reflexes.

He met her angry gaze and noticed she had the most unusual, mesmerizing eyes he'd ever seen. Her eyes were robin's-egg blue, flecked by shades of gold and brown.

"I believe you're trespassing," he said in a calm voice.

"*I'm* trespassing." She frowned. "You're the one who's trespassing. I was invited."

Ty raised his eyebrow. "So was I."

Her delicate golden brows drew together in doubt. "By whom?"

"By my sister. She owns this place."

"Jena's your sister?"

Ty couldn't help the smile that spread across his face at the squeak in her voice. The tinge of embarrassed pink that colored her cheeks was so…sincere.

"Yes. I'm Ty Hudson."

The young woman set the knife back on the plate on the end table before she turned her back to wrap the towel around herself.

Ty grinned at the brief glimpse of her perfect ass. Damn fine one at that.

Turning back to face him, she walked over and kneeled next to him. She untied the electrical cord from around his ankles and said, "Harm invited me to stay here."

Anger sliced through him. "Harm?" It'd only been two months since Harm proposed to Jena. The man better not have a woman on the side or he'd have to kill the bastard.

The woman must've sensed his line of thought, because she quickly filled in the blanks. "Harm had problems with one of Sally's horses. With the wedding days away and Harm's attention otherwise occupied, I volunteered to stay here to keep an eye on the mare and make sure she's healing fine."

As she leaned over him to undo the knot at his wrists, water dripped onto his starched blue dress shirt. Not that he cared. He was too busy enjoying the scent teasing his nostrils—cinnamon and vanilla. Damn, she smelled good. And here he thought cinnamon and apples smelled heavenly. *Her* scent had just blown that theory to smithereens. Ty couldn't help himself. He inhaled once, twice, three times, drinking in her intoxicating aroma.

She looked up at him, concern in her hazel-blue gaze. "Are you okay? Did I tie you too tight?"

When the last of the cord slid off his wrists, she started to pull away. Ty grabbed her left wrist and held her still. He grinned and purposefully lowered his voice to a husky tone. "You're welcome to tie me up anytime you want, gorgeous."

Color bloomed on her cheeks once more, making him realize he hadn't seen such a genuine reaction in a woman in a very long time. His suspicions kicked in. Full force. The woman had to be around twenty-five or so. She couldn't be *that* innocent.

She ignored his comment and stood, using his hold on her wrist to help pull him to his feet.

Once he was back on his feet, Ty's grip loosened on her wrist, yet he still didn't want to release her completely. "You never told me your name." Despite the warning bells going off in his head, he felt a sudden urge to learn everything about this woman.

Evan's heart raced and electricity hummed within her when he slid his fingers slowly down her wrist until his thumb traced the inside of her palm.

Concentrating on answering him instead of the intense physical awareness coursing through her, she was able to focus her mind on responding to his question.

"I'm Evan Masters."

"It's nice to meet you, Miss Masters." Ty lifted her left hand and turned it over, planting a kiss on her open palm.

Her stomach flip-flopped at his intimate kiss. Evan's gaze landed on his short, silky dark hair, skimmed his starched cotton shirt that was stretched across his broad shoulders then moved on to his gray dress slacks and Italian leather shoes. The man's impeccable, expensive clothes reminded her of her own near-naked state and the casual jeans and tank top that awaited her on the bed in the bedroom.

"Er…I hope we can start over. That wasn't the best introduction I've ever given."

His vivid green gaze held a dark, intense look before his eyebrows rose in amusement. "At least I'm now versed in how well you can take care of yourself."

"Sorry about that. My dad made sure I knew how to defend myself."

Ty glanced at the gutted table lamp, the bits of ceramic scattered across the floor and the ripped-out electrical cord that now lay in an innocent tangle on the floor. He met her gaze with an amused one. "I might've gotten knocked off my feet and all tied up by a beautiful woman, but I don't think the lamp fared as well."

For the first time in her life, a man made her body ache all over. Correction…tingle and ache. And this reaction was triggered by nothing more than a complimentary comment and a blatant sexy gaze he cast her way. *My God, what would he be like when he really turned on the charm?*

When he gave her a knowing smile, Evan ground her teeth. Why did she have to be such an easy read?

"Well, it was nice to meet you, Ty." Evan started to back away. "I'll clean the lamp up after I get dressed."

Ty watched Evan bolt from the room and shut the bedroom door behind her. Without her as a distraction, the delicious smell of the apple pie drew his attention once more. He picked up the knife and plate from the end table and carried them into the kitchen. Setting the dirty plate and utensil on the counter, he then crouched next to the sink and opened the two doors underneath it. Yep, the hand broom and dustpan were still in the same spot they were eighteen years ago. During his summer stays, his aunt made sure he knew how to use them, too. Chuckling, Ty grabbed them and walked over to the lamp's mess on the floor.

Once he'd swept up the broken pieces and dumped the rest of the broken lamp and electrical cord into the tall trash can inside the small pantry, Ty opened the cabinet above the counter. He retrieved a clean plate then searched the drawers for a knife and fork.

His mouth watered in anticipation as he cut himself a slice of pie then sat at the kitchen table. When he took that first bite, he closed his eyes at the delicious taste. The flavors of cinnamon and apples blended perfectly. *Jena has really learned to cook over the years*, he thought, remembering all the dinners his sister had botched when they were teens.

"Making yourself at home, I see," Evan's voice sounded from behind him.

Ty turned in the process of taking another bite of pie. The fork paused right before it reached his mouth. "I take it Jena didn't make this pie for me?"

She shook her head, her eyes amused. "But I'm glad to see someone enjoying it. I usually only cook when I'm trying to work something out in my head. I find it therapeutic." She gestured toward him. "Go ahead. You deserve it after cleaning up the mess I made. And now I owe your sister a lamp."

Now that her hair was dry, Ty noted the gorgeous strawberry-blonde color. He smiled his appreciation of her cooking and took another bite. "You make a fantastic apple pie."

Evan grinned and continued into the kitchen. "Thanks. I'm glad you like it."

As she set the backpack she was carrying on the floor next to the chair, his gaze locked on the silver Labrador tag that jostled back and forth against the blue fabric.

He nodded toward her backpack. "Are you an animal lover or something?"

Evan's gaze followed his line of sight to her backpack zipper pull. Her lips quirked upward. "I guess you could say that. I'm...kind of an assistant vet."

"If Harm's horse needs constant attention, why isn't the vet tending to it?"

Evan retrieved another plate and fork. "He's out of town on vacation for a couple of weeks, so I'm filling in for him," she replied as she cut herself a slice of pie and sat down across from him.

"If he trusts you enough to fill in for him, why don't you go to school, get your degree and either open your own practice or partner with him? At least then you'd get all the benefits."

"And all the full-time responsibility!" Evan replied with a chuckle, knowing full well just how much. There was something about this man...she couldn't put her finger on it, but she didn't want him thinking she was some kind of brainiac. If he learned she was the town's vet, he'd question how young she looked. Then he'd inevitably learn she had graduated from high school at sixteen, accelerated through college and moved on to vet school where she entered a dual degree program, earning both her DVM and MBA, before graduating at the young age of twenty-four, and she'd already have a strike against her. In her limited and disappointed experience with men, the male population shied away from women with extremely high IQs.

Just as she was about to take her first bite of pie, her cell phone rang. "Duty calls." Evan gave Ty a half-smile as she jumped up to retrieve her cell phone from her backpack.

She flipped open the cell. "Hello?... Hey, Charlie... When did her water break?... The foal's front hooves aren't coming out first?... No, don't try to turn it yourself. I'll be there in a few minutes. Just try to keep the momma calm."

When she snapped the phone closed, Ty glanced at his watch. "You should consider my suggestion. It seems you're on call 24/7 anyway."

She gave him a wry grin. "I'll take it under advisement." Picking up her backpack, she met his gaze. "I'll collect my things and leave the place to you."

"If Harm invited you, I don't want to kick you out."

"No worries. I'll just drive over each morning and evening." She pulled the house key off her keychain and set it on the table.

"Evan—"

Her cell phone rang again. "Hold that thought." She put up her finger as she flipped open the phone.

"Hello?... Yes, I can squeeze you in. Bring Ranger by the office tomorrow morning. I'll be in at nine."

When she hung up, Ty raised his eyebrow. "I think that vet needs more help."

She grinned and turned to walk toward the bedroom to collect her things, calling over her shoulder, "Yeah, he stays pretty busy."

* * * * *

Three hours later, Evan rolled down her window as she approached her house. Even though Charlie had let her use the shower in his guest bathroom to get cleaned up and she now had on the spare set of clothes she carried around in her car, the scent of birth, sweat, manure and hay still filled her senses. She welcomed the fresh fall night air. The smell brought a nostalgic smile to her lips of skinny-dipping in Sweet Trails Lake and feeling the chill as the fall season cooled down the water a few degrees.

When she saw Chad's pickup truck sitting in her driveway, her stomach tensed and she let out a deep sigh. Pushing on the gas, she drove right past her house. She'd gone out with a Chad twice a couple of months ago. Which was a mistake. She'd been attracted to the fact the man showed no fear of her father. Evan quickly learned Chad's fearlessness had nothing to do with his own bravery, but had everything to do with the fact Chad's father was mayor.

She thought she'd seen confidence in Chad. The truth was, Chad not only thumbed his nose at authority, but he walked around with a cocky confidence that wore off very quickly. He was a good-looking man, but it took more than looks for Evan. She'd turned Chad down when he'd asked her out for a third date. For a man who'd always gotten his way with ladies, Chad seemed to take it as a personal affront that she'd refused to sleep with him.

Ever since then, Chad had periodically shown up and asked her to go out with him. A couple of weeks ago, on the same day she received an invitation to Harm and Jena's wedding, Chad called her and asked her to be his date for the upcoming wedding. So far he didn't seem to want to take "no" for an answer. She didn't feel threatened by Chad in any way—just annoyed—but she had a feeling the guy would hound her about the wedding until she gave in. She knew his ultimate goal—he was damned determined to add her to his list of conquests. She suspected the fact she was a virgin only made her more of a prize in Chad's eyes.

She turned her SUV around in the cul-de-sac at the end of the street and headed back up the road. Hopefully Ty meant what he said about not wanting to kick her out. Sharing a house with the sexy man from Maryland sounded like a great way to remain AWOL for a few more days. She was too busy for Chad to bother at her office.

Once she'd parked her car by the stables, Evan cut the engine and walked into the building to check on Harm's horse, Flash. She unwrapped the horse's hurt leg and massaged the swollen area. While she pressed on the flesh, she was glad she didn't feel any heat that would indicate infection. The swelling was almost gone. In another day, she'd take Flash back to Steele Way for some limited exercise. She knew Flash missed frolicking with the other horses. After tomorrow's jaunt, Evan would be able to tell if Flash was ready to go back to the ranch full-time. She replaced the binding back around Flash's leg and walked out of the stables. Retrieving her backpack from her car, she closed the door with a quiet click.

As she made way to the house, Evan glanced at her watch. It was nine-thirty and the house was dark. Ty must've turned in early. Now she wished she'd held onto the Double D house key. Then she could quietly let herself in without waking Ty. Evan skimmed her gaze over the door. There wasn't a deadbolt, just the main door lock. Setting her backpack on the floor next to her, she unzipped it and pulled out a credit card from her wallet. She'd seen this technique on TV once and wasn't sure if it'd work or not.

Biting her lip, she slid the stiff card between the door and the weather-stripping right where the latch would be. With careful movements, she grasped the doorknob with one hand and maneuvered the credit card with the other until she felt the latch give way.

Evan breathed a sigh of relief that she'd successfully unlocked the door. She shoved her credit card back in her wallet and zipped her backpack closed. Grasping her pack's cloth handle across the top, she turned the doorknob, opened the door and stepped inside.

The cool air-conditioning caused chill bumps to form on her arms. Sheesh, the man must run very hot. *Now there's an intriguing idea,* she thought with a wicked grin. Her lower belly tightened at the thought, but Evan didn't have time to ponder any more because someone grabbed her neck and slammed her back against the open front door.

Reacting on pure instinct, Evan dropped her bag and brought her knee up, expecting to nail her attacker in the groin. Instead she met a hard muscular thigh as the man blocked her move.

"Evan? Are you trying to get yourself killed?" Ty hissed in the dark. He released her neck and encircled her bare arms in a tight grip.

Her eyes quickly adjusted to the moonlight filtering through the front door. Ty stood in front of her wearing only his gray dress pants and an intense look on his face. Her gaze slid down his tightly cut chest to his trim, well-defined abs.

"I was trying not to wake you. I didn't expect to be attacked," she shot back while her heart slammed against her rib cage. Evan appreciated a nice body with the best of them, but more than anything else Ty's scent caught her attention. She took a deep breath. He smelled so good, like sandalwood and musky male.

Ty's grip on her arms loosened and he took a step closer. His fingers slowly trailed down her arms and a half-smile tilted the corners of his lips. He glanced at her tank top's spaghetti straps as if he wanted to plant a kiss on her shoulder. "I thought you said you were going home."

The husky timbre of his voice made her heart rate rev. Ty stood a good four inches taller than her five-foot-ten height. Perfect, she thought as her stomach fluttered at his nearness. The man made her senses come alive. There was just something about his quiet, intense approach that made her tingle all over. He exuded self-confidence without conscious effort. The combination was so devastating to her senses she couldn't help but be affected by his nearness.

"Um, something came up and I decided if you didn't mind sharing a house with me for a couple of days, I'd stay."

"I like my privacy." A frown creased his brow and his expression turned serious.

Her stomach pitched and disappointment rushed through her. She started to pick up the bag she'd dropped. "Okay, I'll leave—"

The pressure of Ty's fingers on her chin caused her to pause and meet his gaze.

"But I've been known to make exceptions."

The deep register of his voice followed by his fingers skimming down her neck sent a shiver of heated response down her spine and straight to her core.

"Is that an invitation?" She knew her voice sounded breathless, but she didn't care.

"Tell me why you're hiding out here. Maybe I can help."

His seductive low tone drew her in. Evan's breath caught at the heat she felt emanating off his skin. This sexy man was giving her exactly what she wanted, the beginnings of an attraction between a man and a woman. No preconceived notions. No worry that she could run circles around him on an IQ level…nothing but pure and honest desire zinged between them. The way he made her feel—breathless and totally caught up—she realized he was the perfect man to lose her virginity to. He was only temporarily in Texas, so it's not like he would think she'd expect anything more than a weekend from him.

He put his hand on the door behind her and leaned a bit closer. "Tell me what changed your mind."

His encouraging, calm voice made her feel so comfortable with him.

Evan placed her hands tentatively on his bare chest. She couldn't resist, he was so gorgeous. When her skin touched his, his warmth shot straight to her toes.

"I just prefer to avoid an old boyfriend who's determined to have me as his date at your sister's wedding. Once the wedding's over, he'll stop hounding me."

Ty narrowed his gaze for a brief moment as if he knew there was more to what she told him. Then he pulled her away from the door. "Looks like we'll be sharing quarters for a few days." Picking up the backpack she'd dropped when he'd grabbed her, he followed her inside and kicked the door closed with his foot.

Evan stood in the dark, facing Ty. A pregnant silence stretched for a long, heated moment. The attraction arcing between them wove through the air making her aware of every breath she took.

"I'll take the couch," she offered.

"I think it'll be a tight fit."

"Huh?"

"That's where I'm sleeping. You can have the bed."

"I don't want to kick you out of your bed, Ty."

"You could always join me." His gaze locked with hers, his suggestion blatant and honest.

Her heart galloped. Was he teasing her? It was hard to tell with his serious expression. "Um, I'll take the bed."

The corners of his lips tilted in amusement at her quick response. Handing her the bag, he said in a husky tone, "Sleep well."

Evan's fingers accidentally brushed his when she took the backpack. Her heart leapt and her breath hitched at the contact. She quickly glanced at him, hoping he hadn't heard.

Ty's penetrating gaze slid down her face, lingered at her breasts then returned to her lips. "See you in the morning."

Even in the dim light, the heated look in his eyes told her he wanted to follow her to the bedroom. Heaven help her, she wanted him to. How could she be so attracted to a complete stranger?

She took a steadying breath to calm the rapid beating of her heart. "Thank you for your generosity. Good night." Then she turned and walked into the bedroom.

Once Evan closed the bedroom door, Ty stretched out on the couch and folded his arms behind his head, contemplating her. Generosity? He chuckled at her comment. He was a selfish bastard through and through.

He could still smell her sweet vanilla and cinnamon scent, feel her warm body pressed to his, her generous breasts crushed against his chest while her heart beat at a rapid pace. He didn't think it'd take much to seduce Evan, but for some reason he didn't want to push her too fast. Maybe he liked anticipating just how she'd feel when he slid inside her. She was the perfect height, allowing for all kinds of sexual positions. His groin throbbed at the thought.

Evan looked nothing like the sophisticated women he normally slept with, yet there was something about her natural look…gorgeous shoulder-length wavy strawberry-blonde hair, wide-set sexy blue-brown eyes combined with the sprinkle of freckles across her nose made him hard as a rock as soon as he laid eyes on her. Not to mention she had a body he definitely wanted to explore from head to toe.

The blush he'd seen on her cheeks when he saw her naked made him think she hadn't had many sexual partners. Yet her self-confidence told him she'd probably be open to just about anything he dished out. A slow smile curved his lips as he unzipped his pants and stroked his cock to full, rigid attention.

When he was almost at peak, Ty closed his eyes and focused on taking deep, even breaths until his erection diminished. He welcomed the biting challenge to his body just as he looked forward to exploring anything and everything Evan would allow while he pushed her to the limits of her sexual bounds. The woman had no idea just what kind of man she was sharing a house with. He learned a long time ago to leave his emotions and his conscience at the door. "No inhibitions, no limits" was a motto he'd lived by.

He frowned when he thought of how quickly she'd tied him and shoved that knife in his face. Her confidence and sassy attitude didn't mesh with the story she told him about her old boyfriend. He intuitively knew she wasn't the kind of woman to hide from her problems. He'd find out the truth soon enough.

Chapter Two

Evan awoke to a very quiet house. The sun was just peeking out over the horizon. Once she had her morning cup of coffee, she'd feed and check on Flash. Maybe she'd take her for a slow walk today.

Evan slid into a pair of blue jeans and a baby blue tank top then pulled her wavy hair back into a quick ponytail. As she brushed her teeth, she critiqued her face in the mirror. She had big, wide-set eyes, her best feature as far as she was concerned. The unusual color combination tended to draw people's attention. Her nose was passable, not too big or too small, but she had a nice mouth. "Full lips," Chad had called them. The few times he'd kissed her, he tried to suck them.

She removed her toothbrush from her mouth and took in her overall look. She was a farm-bred cowgirl from her wavy hair to the tips of her toes. All she was missing was her cowboy hat and boots. What would city-bred Ty, with his expensive, starched cotton shirts, silk-blend pants and Italian leather shoes, see in her?

She frowned as she spit the toothpaste in the sink then stuck her tongue out at herself in the mirror.

Nothing.

Disappointed, she turned to walk out of the bathroom and caught a glimpse of her jeans-encased rear in the mirror. Then again, Ty could be an ass man. A broad smile replaced her frown. *Work with what you've got, girl*, she told herself as she flipped the light switch off.

Evan was surprised to find the living room empty. *Where could Ty be?* she wondered as she made her way to the kitchen and pulled out a bag of ground coffee from the cabinet.

Staring through the white linen curtains over the sink, she peered out the window. Ty's rental car was still parked in front of the house. Then she saw movement to her right that drew her attention. Ty stood thirty feet away, facing the rising sun. His chest and feet were bare, but he still wore the pants he had on yesterday. He moved with precise hand and foot actions as if he were doing some kind of solo martial arts practice.

Evan's breath caught as she watched his fluid movements. She had to tear her gaze away to measure the coffee into the filter, add water and turn the coffeepot on.

The smell of fresh-brewed coffee wafted through the air along with the sound of the coffee filling the pot. Evan inhaled, enjoying the rich scent. As much as she loved coffee, she often thought it smelled better brewing than it actually tasted…at least until she added cream and sugar, she mentally amended with a smile as she opened the cabinet and reached up to pull down a coffee cup.

Just as her hand gripped the ceramic cup, warm fingers surrounded hers at the same time. Ty laid his chest against her back. Wow, how'd he get inside so fast, and without her hearing him enter?

"This has to be the sexiest backside I've seen in a very long time," he whispered in her ear while he lowered their hands, cup and all, to the counter. "Morning, Evan."

A shiver coursed through her at his seductive comment. Evan stared at his hand covering hers around the cup. She literally felt his heat from her shoulders to the base of her spine. His musky scent made her body heat up all over.

When he pulled away, she turned to face him and raised an eyebrow at the sheen of sweat that coated his chest and dampened the fringes of his close-cropped hair.

"You were working out?"

He flashed her a smile then nodded toward the coffeepot. "You make enough for me?"

Evan retrieved another coffee cup and filled it to the brim. Intuitively she knew this man took his coffee black. As she handed him the cup and watched him take his first sip, Evan took in his well-defined abs in the early morning light and her stomach fluttered. What would it feel like to have those abs pressed against her in more than just a teasing manner? The fact he worked out in his dress pants, not caring a whit that he sweated all over the expensive material surprised her. Was there a bit of the country boy in Ty? Come to think of it…why had he worked out in his dress pants?

She gestured with her empty cup toward him. "You work out in your dress clothes often?"

Ty glanced down at his attire and grimaced. "Only when my rental car is stolen with my suitcase in it."

"Oh, sorry. I didn't know."

Ty took a sip of his coffee and leaned against the counter. "I just hope they find the car and my suitcase soon or I'll be doing some shopping."

Once he finished speaking, Evan realized Ty was staring at her over his coffee cup. Those green eyes seemed to read so much, to stare right though her, picking up her innermost thoughts and doubts. Turning back to the coffeepot, she murmured, "Why don't you sit down and I'll make us some breakfast."

"Got something on your mind?"

"What?" she asked as she turned back to see his dark eyebrow elevated in amusement.

A flush stole over her cheeks at his reminder she'd told him she cooked when she was mulling over something. "I'm just hungry. I figured feeding you is the least I can do for you allowing me to stay here."

The look in Ty's eyes shifted and the green color turned darker. "I look forward to tasting what you offer up," he said in a husky tone before he turned and sat down at the table.

"Just sit tight. I'll have breakfast done in no time," she said in a bright voice. Her heart racing, Evan turned back to the stove and withdrew the skillet from the drawer below. The man was just too sexy for words. God, he was way out of her league. She was insane to think she'd have anything to offer him. Sure, she knew her own body, but she was inexperienced when it came to knowing what a man wanted...well, other than to get off as fast as he possibly could. Was that written in a how-to-be-a-man manual somewhere?

She opened the fridge and retrieved the bacon, then laid a few pieces of meat in the hot skillet, her mind whirling. But the good part was...if she made a fool of herself, Ty wouldn't be around to remind her of it. No matter how tense she felt over bringing the subject up with Ty, she refused to talk herself out of this idea. While she turned the bacon with a fork, she felt even more certain Ty was perfect—in every since of the word. The man obviously wanted to pursue something with her. She'd be a fool not to take him up on it.

Once she'd set the cooked bacon on a napkin-lined plate, Evan pulled out the carton of eggs from the fridge and cracked a few eggs in the pan. While she scrambled the eggs with a spatula, her confidence built. She knew she was making the right decision.

After she'd placed the plate and silverware in front of him, Ty picked up his fork and dug into the food with gusto, commenting, "I don't usually eat such a large breakfast."

Evan sat down across from him with her own plate and utensils. She picked up her fork. "Me either. I'm usually too busy."

"With your job?" Ty asked as he popped a forkful of eggs into his mouth.

She took a bite of her bacon and nodded.

After he swallowed, Ty tilted his head to the side, contemplating her. "Why don't you go back to school and get your vet license? Then you can open up your own business."

That was the second time he mentioned she strive to own the veterinary business. He seemed really bothered by the fact she deserved more out of her job, that she wasn't working to her full potential. Then again, from his comments to her about her own career, Ty appeared to be the type of man who worked hard, strove to be at the top of the ladder, no matter the odds. She'd lay money on the fact he owned his own business.

"So what do you do?"

Ty picked up a piece of bacon and bit into it. "I'm part owner of an architecture firm in Maryland."

Bingo! "Ah, I was right."

His brow creased. "About what?"

She smiled. "That you're a very driven, career-minded person."

"And that's a bad thing?"

"Not at all. I was just making a comment."

"You're right. I'm very driven to reach my goals." His voice dropped to a seductive purr. "In every aspect in my life."

She couldn't miss the sexual connotation of his tone. Well, this was as good a time as any, Evan thought as she took a breath. "About the offer you made to help me last night…"

Ty's fork paused on the way to his mouth. He raised an eyebrow, his expression intrigued.

She plowed forward before she lost her courage. "I could use your help in one area. You know the boyfriend I told you about?"

Ty nodded.

"I think you could help get him off my back once and for all."

"How can I help you?" he asked before he took another bite of eggs.

"You can sleep with me."

Ty's gaze jerked to hers and he choked on his food.

Alarmed, Evan jumped up and came around the table to touch his shoulder. "Are you okay?"

Still coughing, Ty nodded and met her concerned gaze. "You want me to have sex with you to get rid of your boyfriend?"

She gave a half-laugh at the way it sounded coming from Ty. "I guess that sounded weird, huh?"

He grabbed her around the waist and pulled her into his lap. "Baby, I'll be more than happy to accommodate you, but I have to know why my having sex with you would make your old boyfriend leave you alone."

Relief flooded through her that Ty had said yes. Placing her hands on his broad shoulders, Evan laughed. "Getting rid of this blasted virginity once and for all should make Chad go away. I think he sees my virginity as some kind of trophy to notch into his bedpost. So once it's gone, he'll just see me as any other woman and move on."

As soon as she said the word "virginity", Evan felt Ty's shoulders tense.

Ty set her back on the floor and adopted a tense expression. "I'm sorry, but I don't 'do' virgins."

His rejection hit her like a slap in the face. Evan's ire rose when she noted the muscle jumping in his jaw and the fact he wasn't looking at her any longer. She knew the man was fighting his desire. Damn him. He still wanted her, even if he had some hang-up against virgins. No way was she going to let him put a brick wall between them because of it. If he wanted to see her meet her full potential, the man was about to find out just how determined she could be when she set her mind to something.

She crossed her arms. "What's wrong, Ty? You have something against virgins?"

He met her gaze head-on, anger flashing in the deep green depths. "Virgins expect commitment and I'm not a commitment kind of guy."

"No worries there, big guy. I only asked you because you're here for the short-term."

Something flared in Ty's gaze. Interest? Was he caving? She'd damn well make sure he did. She had a feeling this man couldn't resist a challenge.

Evan put her hands on her hips. "Tell ya what. How about a little wager? I challenge you to a wresting match. If you pin me for ten seconds, I'll drop my request. But if I win, you'll follow through."

Ty's eyes narrowed, suspicion reflected in his gaze.

"Surely you don't think you'll lose?" She couldn't help but add the dig.

A broad grin spread across Ty's face as he stood to his full height. Staring down at her, he said in low tone, "I'm going to enjoy pinning you."

She tilted her chin at his cocky comment. "You forget so quickly who had whom trussed up like a pig yesterday."

Ty raised a dark eyebrow then swept his arm toward the living room where they'd have a little space. "You're welcome to try your best, Miss."

Evan preceded him into the living room and quickly became irritated at the formal tone he'd adopted, as if he were already distancing himself from her. Her narrowed gaze tracked Ty as he moved the sofa and chair back to give them room.

Ty approached her then walked around her in a slow circle as if he were stalking his prey. She didn't give him the satisfaction of seeing her gaze trace his steps behind her. She knew he was there, waiting.

"Are you ready?" Ty's deep voice came from directly behind her.

She didn't respond. Instead, she swiftly dropped to a squat and swept her leg behind her, hooking his ankles.

Ty stumbled, but kept his footing. "Nice try."

He grinned at her once she'd straightened and faced him. "Are you going to tell me why you're still a virgin at…what are you? Twenty-six?"

They each circled, looking for a weak spot.

"Yes, I'm twenty-six and why I'm still a virgin is none of your damn business." Evan lunged at him, trying to take him off balance.

He used her momentum against her and before she knew what had happened she was flat on her back on the rug. Ty's body covered hers. He had her pinned.

Evan tried to use her legs to shove him off her, but Ty wrapped his legs around hers, locking them in place. His naked chest pressed against her thin T-shirt, making her very aware of his heat and his sexy smell.

The amused look fled his face, replaced by a serious one when he met her annoyed gaze. "You can tell me now."

"It's not important. Let me up."

Ty peered into her eyes for a long moment as if he debated whether to push the issue. "Not until you say Uncle."

Annoyed he'd so thoroughly bested her, Evan began to squirm in earnest to be released. Did he *have* to rub it in?

He just held her tighter. "Go ahead, Evan…say Uncle."

"No," she yelled, exerting herself once more.

Ty was amazed at Evan's tenacity and the stubborn streak that ran through the woman. She felt so good underneath him. Why the hell did she have to be a blasted virgin?

"You're so damn stubborn. Concede. Say Uncle."

Anger flushed her face. She shook her head and started to speak as if she were going to say "no" when something in her eyes changed and she said, "Daddy!"

Ty chuckled. "I'm just ten years older than you, so 'uncle' will do."

Then he heard someone clear his throat behind him. Ty glanced over his shoulder to see a tall, broad-shouldered, salt-and-pepper-haired man in his fifties. He stood there with his arms crossed and a deep scowl on his face.

And then Ty saw the morning sunlight reflect off the sheriff's badge on the man's chest. If the situation weren't so damn tense, it'd be funny.

"There better be a damn good reason you have my daughter held to the floor."

Ty quickly let go of Evan and stood, pulling her to her feet. "Good morning, Sheriff," he said, extending his hand.

The sheriff ignored his hand and pinned his gaze on Evan. "What are you doing here, Evelyn?"

She walked into her father's open arms and gave her dad a hug, then peered into his face. "I could ask you the same thing."

"I'm here on business." Her dad frowned. When he flicked his gaze to Ty, his frown deepened.

"Me too," she shot back with a grin.

Ty almost choked when the sheriff's gaze narrowed.

Evan looked at Ty and then her dad. "Ty, this is my father, Jake Masters. Dad, this is Ty Hudson, Jena's brother."

"I know who he is," her dad said, looking at Ty. "I'm here to tell you we've found your stolen rental car. I'll take you to town, and we'll get all the paperwork straightened out and release your belongings to you."

Glancing at his daughter, he continued in a suspicious voice, "Why are you here so early in the morning?"

"Because I'm st—"

"She's here to look after Harm's horse," Ty intervened in a calm tone. The last thing he needed was a sheriff arresting him for living in sin with his daughter.

The sheriff cut his gaze to Evan. "You are?"

She nodded. "I promised Harm I'd look out for Flash until she's able to go back with the other horses."

"I hope he's paying you double-time," her father grumbled.

She reached up and kissed him on the cheek. "But of course."

The sheriff's dark brown gaze returned to Ty where he assessed Ty's half-dressed appearance with clear disapproval. He started to speak again when Evan said, "Why don't you get dressed, Ty. Then you can follow Dad to town in your rental car and collect your stuff."

The sheriff crossed his arms and his lips lifted in a cold smile. "I don't mind taking Ty to town and bringing him back to the Double D. As a matter of fact, I insist on it."

I'm sure he'll love driving me to town, Ty thought as he grabbed his shirt from the sofa and walked into the bedroom. *Great. Just what I need…an angry, overprotective father drilling me about my intentions with his daughter all the way to the station.*

* * * * *

"What are your intentions with my daughter?" Jake said as soon as they started down the drive toward the main road.

Yep, he'd known it was coming. Ty almost sighed out loud. "Pardon?"

"You heard me."

Ty narrowed his gaze at the man's brisk tone. "I'm just here for my sister's wedding, Sheriff."

"Evan's a virgin," Jake said as if he hadn't spoken.

"And just why the hell is Evan's sex life or lack thereof everyone's business?" Ty snapped, more than a little annoyed for Evan's sake. Obviously he wasn't the only guy the sheriff had shared this information with.

"Because she's my little girl," the sheriff countered as if that answered everything.

"What Evan chooses to do or not do with her sex life is up to her and no one else."

Jake's dark eyebrows drew together at Ty's open challenge. "You've got some brass ones. I'll give you that. But mine are bigger. Her mother died when Evan was ten. She's all I've got in my life and no one is going to screw with her…either literally or figuratively."

Ty glanced away, peering out the window. Why did he even say anything? It wasn't like he was going to take Evan up on her proposition. But for some reason, the fact the whole damn town was probably aware of Evan's virginity bugged the shit out of him. No wonder she wanted to get the hell rid of it. It'd become a thorn in her side instead of a special gift to give the right man in her life. Glancing at her overbearing father, he knew exactly why Evan was still a virgin. In such a small town, no one would go against the sheriff without putting a ring on her finger.

No one, except me, his subconscious finished the thought even if he never planned to act on it.

* * * * *

"Hey, big brother," Jena said as she ran up and hugged him tight. Ty gave her a bear hug and twirled her around. He didn't realize how much he'd miss seeing his sister until she moved to Texas a couple of months ago.

"It's great to see you, too." Setting Jena on the ground he looped his arm across her shoulders as he shook Harm's outstretched hand. "Good to see you again, Harm. You ready to stop living in sin with my sister?"

"Ty! We waited for *you*." Jena jabbed him in the ribs with her elbow then moved over to hug Harm's waist.

Harm kissed her on the temple and pulled her close, a wide grin on his face. "Hell yeah, I'm ready," he replied as he tilted his Stetson back.

"What took you so long to get here this morning?"

Ty took in his sister's rosy cheeks, the highlights in her blonde hair lightened even more by the Texas sun. His sister was truly happy. His gut tightened a little at the thought she'd be permanently so far away. He'd just have to make an effort to visit her a couple of times a year.

"The sheriff showed up this morning to let me know my rental car had been recovered along with my stuff."

"I'm really sorry about your car getting stolen. What rotten luck."

"Yeah, Texas seems to do that to me," he said in a wry tone.

"Well, I'm glad you're settled at the Double D. At least you'll have the privacy you like so much," she teased.

"Um, you said Ty could stay at your aunt's house?" A concerned expression crossed Harm's face.

Jena glanced up at her fiancé. "Yes, why?"

Harm gave her a sheepish look, "Well, 'cause I told Evan she could use the house while she was taking care of Flash."

"Oh." Jena's gaze jerked to her brother.

Ty shook his head. "Don't worry. We've worked it out. Evan owes you a lamp, but other than that…"

Amusement danced in his sister's gaze. "A lamp? Do I want to know?"

"Not really." Ty gave a half-laugh. "I'm only here for the wedding so it's not a big deal."

"But there's only one bed."

"There's also a couch," Ty reminded his sister.

Harm grinned. "Oh yeah, the couch…"

Jena blushed bright red at Harm's suggestive tone. "Okay, that's enough. I'm convinced. As long as you and Evan are okay with it."

Ty shoved his hands in his jeans' pockets. "No problem. So what are the plans for the next couple of days?"

* * * * *

Ty stood in the shower, rinsing off the day's grime. Jena and Harm were having a long overdue engagement party tonight at one of the local bars called Rockin' Joe's. Jena said they'd waited to have it so he could attend.

He'd hung with his sister and Harm all day, helping with chores on their ranch. His shoulders ached from all the bales of hay he'd helped lift. Even though he exercised regularly, he'd used muscles today that he didn't necessarily exert on a regular basis. He'd forgotten how good it felt to work on a ranch.

At the end of the day, he'd ignored the heat and taken a long ride of one of Harm's stallions. Damn, that was an awesome rush. It'd been a helluva long time since he'd felt so free, galloping in the hot wind out on an open range.

As the warm water slid down his body, Ty's mind wandered to Evan. What had she done today? He'd been a little disappointed to find her car gone when he arrived back at the house. Even though he had no plans of seducing her, Ty couldn't help but remember how her sweet body felt pressed against his. When he closed his eyes, he smelled her vanilla and cinnamon scent. He pictured her naked and wet…like she'd been yesterday. But this time she was in the shower with him. He'd pull her close and inhale the soft skin of her neck then kiss the sensitive spot where her shoulder met her throat.

She'd moan and his balls would tighten at the sexy sound. His erection hardened instantly at the turn in his train of thought.

Ty placed a hand on the shower wall while he grasped his rigid cock. He imagined how good Evan would feel pressed against him, how warm and wet and so damn tight she'd be when he slid inside her. He gritted his teeth at the sensations his mind conjured as he stroked his erection. As much as he preferred women who'd had lots of experience in bed, Evan's innocence combined with her guileless nature attracted him on so many levels.

His lower stomach muscles tightened as he came close to peak. Ty took deep breaths to halt his climax just before he came. Damn, the anticipation felt good. Focused concentration and flexing his lower muscles worked every time. His shoulder and chest muscles relaxed as he took a few more calming breaths then gripped his cock once more.

A cool breeze hitting his wet skin caused his eyes to snap open. He saw the shower curtain fall back into place at the same time he made out Evan's form exiting the bathroom.

Ty's chest tightened in heightened sexual response to the realization she'd been watching him. Unabashed curiosity and innocence…what a fucking alluring combination! The thought caused his erection to fill full of blood, harder than it had been. His balls pulled tight in anticipation.

He imagined pressing Evan against the shower wall, cupping her sweet ass and lifting her so he could bury himself in her warm sheath. Ty grasped his cock tighter then slammed his fist straight to the base while he let go of the physical control he'd been holding back. He groaned at the explosive climax that ricocheted through his body. He came in long, hard bursts, his body's physical response making his hips jerk in rapid succession.

As his movements slowed, Ty knew that if he had Evan in the shower with him right now, he'd relish every sensation from the hot water pounding on them, to the feel of her soft skin pressed against his to her vanilla and cinnamon smell. The sound of her moans mixed with his while their soap-coated bodies slid against each other would be an incredibly visceral experience.

Too bad he didn't plan to go there.

Chapter Three

Evan's cheeks flushed as she exited the bathroom, not in embarrassment, but in sheer sexual excitement. She'd watched the water sluice over Ty's broad shoulders and down his cut chest and abs. Her gaze had locked on his hand around his erection. The man not only had a body to die for, but he was also exceptionally well-endowed. She might be a virgin but growing up a tomboy, she'd seen enough cocks to know the difference.

As she left the house and headed for the barn, her mind replayed the scene she'd just witnessed. Watching Ty slide his hand down his erection, taking himself to the edge only to expend mental and physical effort to hold back his orgasm, was the most erotic sight she'd ever witnessed. What had possessed her to peek, she had no clue. Ty was like a magnet she couldn't resist being drawn to. Before he opened his eyes, she left as quickly as she could. Thank God. She didn't know what she would've said or done if he'd opened his eyes to see her standing there watching him.

When she entered the stall, Flash danced around, excited to see her. Evan checked the horse's leg, then patted her neck and whispered in her ear, "You're antsy, aren't ya, girl?" This time Evan left the bandage off. Flash was better today. Maybe some fresh air would do her some good. Evan knew some fresh air was something she could use, too.

After she'd saddled Flash, Evan took her out in the pasture behind the barn where the mare moved from a walk to a trot. Flash had been cooped up in the stall in the final stages of healing from her leg injury for the past couple of days. Up until today, Evan had allowed the healing horse short walks, but she felt Flash was ready and antsy for more. As the wind blew through her hair and her body moved with the horse's movements, Evan's heart raced and her sex ached at the arousing situation she'd just witnessed from Ty. She'd known he was getting ready to make himself come. Sexual frustration welled within her. Damn, she needed her own release soon.

* * * * *

Evan arrived at Rockin' Joe's just after eight. Harm and Jena's engagement party started at seven. Go figure, she was always late. But people had come to expect that of her. The nature of her job had her on constant on-call status.

Harm and Jena had rented out the entire place, so everyone there was an invited guest. She was glad they'd decided to have their engagement party in a casual atmosphere like Rockin' Joe's. She tugged at the hem of her baby pink tank top and straightened her silver and turquoise belt buckle at the waist of her jeans as she glanced around the crowded bar. Since her mother died when she was young, Evan grew into adulthood without a close female influence. Needless to say that left her with a wardrobe full of jeans, tank tops, T-shirts, boots and little else.

To Evan, being "dressed to kill" meant she wore her hair down, and her shiny boots, not her scuffed ones. She glanced down at the scuffed boots on her feet with a wry smile. Her hair fell toward her face with her movements. She tossed the strawberry-blonde loose waves away from her face as she lifted her head. At least she wore her hair down tonight.

Her dad and uncle were talking to Harm and Jena next to the bar. She'd catch up with them later when she gave Harm an update on Flash.

She waved to Colt Tanner and his brothers Mace and Cade. They were standing near a corner booth drinking beers. Cade must've come home briefly from his rodeo touring, she thought with a grin as Mace picked up a beer from the table. He made his way over to her and handed her the longneck.

"How's it going, Evan?" he asked over the loud country music.

Evan took the beer and met Mace's hazel-green gaze. The man had one of the sexiest smiles she'd ever seen. He always knew how to make a person feel welcome and, if that person happened to be a female, wanted.

"What's the beer for?"

He laughed then glanced at his watch. "I knew you'd be late, 'bout an hour. Thought I'd have a drink ready for you when you got here so you could catch up with the rest of us."

"Thanks for keeping me up to speed." Evan grinned as she took a sip of her beer.

Out of the corner of her eye, Evan saw Chad shouldering his way through the crowd toward her, a determined look on his face. The man was six feet four and built like a linebacker, so he was hard to miss in a crowd. Her heart jerked and her stomach tensed. She didn't want to deal with him tonight. Grabbing Mace's hand, she said in a bright voice, "Come on, let's dance."

Mace followed her line of sight, then grinned and laced his fingers with hers. "Still hounding ya?"

"Like a dog going after his favorite bone." She rolled her eyes and tugged him toward the dance floor, her boot heels making a thudding sound on the wood underneath her feet.

Mace took her beer and set it on a table before they stepped into the dance floor area. Garth Brooks' "Rodeo" was blaring from the speakers and Evan couldn't help but tease Mace as he pulled her against his hard chest. "I should be dancing this song with Cade."

He flashed her a devil-may-care smile. "Cade's not the dancing sort, darlin'. You know I'm a helluva lot more fun."

Evan laughed at Mace's self-confident comment as they began to dance. The man always made her smile.

"Evan." Chad's voice sounded behind them. Her stomach tensed.

"She's dancin' at the moment." Mace gave him a direct, penetrating look.

"I'm talking to Evan, not you," Chad challenged Mace.

Evan felt Mace's shoulders tense underneath her fingers. She glanced at Chad. "Chad, as Mace said, I'm dancing right now."

Chad's hand landed on her shoulder. He turned her to face him. "Not anymore you're not. We need to talk."

Mace grabbed Chad's upper arm. His expression turned serious. "I think you need to take a break, champ."

"Get the hell off me." Chad scowled at the same time he shrugged Mace's hand off his arm.

Running his hand through his dark blond hair, Chad continued, his expression angry as he addressed Evan once more, "Where were you last night?"

Evan felt several pairs of eyes turn their way. People had stopped dancing around them. Damn, Chad was making a scene. She didn't want to spoil Harm and Jena's party. Maybe if she just walked outside to talk to him, he'd leave her alone.

Stepping out of Mace's arms, she started to say, "Let's go outside, Chad..."

Ty walked up beside Mace and spoke in a calm tone, "I believe the lady said she isn't interested in talking."

"Who the hell are you?" Chad all but yelled at Ty.

"I'm the man she was with last night," Ty replied. His green gaze narrowed on Chad, daring him to say another word.

Evan's cheeks flooded with color at Ty's casual comment. A hush spread throughout the crowd. Even the music had stopped...or had the song just ended?

Oh boy!

Shock crossed Chad's face then sheer fury replaced his surprised expression. He took a swing at Ty. "She's mine."

Evan blinked when she realized Chad was lying facedown on the floor. How in the world had that happened so fast? Ty had Chad's arm bent back at a strange angle, keeping him down.

Ty had moved so quickly and with such fluid movements she realized he'd disabled Chad in less than two seconds flat.

Heavy boot heels stomped across the wooden dance floor. "Do I need to get involved?" the sheriff's voice boomed near them.

Ty glanced up at her father then down at Chad before he released him. "No, I think he was just leaving."

Chad scrambled to his feet. "You should arrest him for assault." He scowled as he rubbed his shoulder.

Jake narrowed his gaze on Chad. "You'd better leave before I forget I'm the sheriff and follow my fatherly instincts."

Chad met his own father's gaze as the mayor walked up behind the sheriff.

"Dad?"

The tall man nodded his silver head. "Go on, son. We don't want to spoil Harm and Jena's evening."

"I still want to talk to you," Chad said to Evan before he turned on his boot heel and left the bar.

Her father gave Ty a curt nod then he focused his gaze on Evan. "Until we put a security system in your house, you shouldn't leave your home unattended at night."

His comment came across loud and clear. He didn't want her staying at the ranch house. Period.

Evan lifted her chin a notch. No one told her what to do. Not even her father.

The song "Shameless" by Garth Brooks had just started up and before she could comment, Ty took her hand. "I believe you said I owe you a dance."

Evan's gaze darted between Ty and her father. She felt a need to assert her independence, but the thought of being held close to Ty offered major appeal. She glanced at Mace who winked and said, "You have to grant your rescuer at least one dance."

Her father raised his eyebrow, but didn't say a word before he turned away. The crowd around them had begun to dance once more. As Mace walked away, Ty wrapped his arms around her waist and pulled her flush against his hard chest. Evan closed her eyes for a second and relished the sensation of being surrounded by Ty's strength, his heat and his seductive smell.

Sighing her approval, her gaze landed on his open-necked, button-down shirt. Today he looked very much "the cowboy" with his jeans, chambray shirt and boots. If it weren't for his Maryland accent, she could easily mistake Ty for a Texas cowboy, born and bred. It was the way he carried himself. He exuded sheer masculine confidence in every movement he made.

"I don't know if I should punch you or kiss you for what you did. Either way, thanks," she whispered in his ear. The man had gone up against her father. That took some big *cojones*.

"Chad's a prick," he commented, his breath warm against her neck.

Evan closed her eyes once more and imagined that Ty wanted to hold her in his arms instead of the fact he'd asked her to dance to head off an argument between her father and her. Why did Ty have to have some stupid rule against sleeping with virgins?

She remembered the shower water sluicing over his gorgeous, naked body and the sight of him in full arousal. The thought made her shiver in sexual awareness. Of course, her desire probably had to do with the fact the man also really knew how to dance. He matched her movements, step for step, making sure to keep their bodies flush against one another. From his intense charisma to his natural rhythm, Ty made her feel breathless, needy and so incredibly turned on.

When Ty's lips grazed her neck, she gasped in surprise and her eyes flew open, locking with his steady gaze.

His fingers tightened on her waist before he lowered his hands to her hips. Pulling her hips forward, he fit her body even closer to his. A serious expression had settled on his face. "I'll take the virginity you so willingly offered, but we're going to do it my way."

"Your way?" She was barely able to breathe, her heart beat so rapidly in her chest. The thought of having Ty's naked body gliding against hers made her breasts ache and her lower stomach muscles tense in aroused anticipation.

His warm hands slid up her waist to her upper back. He applied pressure on her back until her chest was pressed against his. His mouth hovered a breath away as his gaze collided with hers. He gave her a feral smile. "Yeah, my way."

Unable to form a coherent response, Evan nodded her assent.

The song ended and Ty stepped away from her. "I'll see you back at the Double D."

Evan spent the rest of the evening going through the motions of socializing. Ty's agreement had left her body on a tightly wound spring. She was so aroused at the thought of being with the sexy man that she thought for sure if someone touched her she'd go up in flames. Finally, after being at the party for a good hour and a half, she made her way over to Harm and Jena.

"Hey, you two. Nice party."

A look of concern crossed Jena's face. "You okay, Evan?"

Evan knew she referred to the scene Chad caused earlier. She shrugged. "Sure. I'm sorry about that."

Harm wrapped an arm around Jena's shoulders. "No need to apologize, Evan. Chad was outta line."

"Yeah. I had no idea my brother knew martial arts. Speaking of which…" Jena paused as she glanced around the room. "Did he leave already?"

Harm nodded. "He told me he'd see us tomorrow at the ranch."

"You going to put him to work again?" Jena laughed, amusement reflected in her gaze as she looked up at her husband-to-be.

"Hell yeah. If I've got a hardworking man like Ty at my disposal for a few days, I could always use the extra pair of hands."

Jena winked. "He loves it."

Harm's dark brown gaze met Evan's. "If Flash is finally up to speed, I'll come get her tomorrow."

Evan shook her head. "I'm not sure if she's ready to be out on the range by herself yet. I took her for a trot earlier today. She seemed to enjoy that. I'll bring her by Steele Way and let her visit for an hour or so. Then I'll take her back for a couple more nights. I just want to be sure she's fully recovered. Babysitting an injured horse is the last thing you should be doing right now with all your wedding stuff going on."

Harm smiled his appreciation. He rubbed his jaw as he glanced at Jena. "It just occurred to me that Ty might want a horse while he's at the Double D."

Evan grinned. "No problem. I'll bring Flash by tomorrow in my two-sided trailer. Then I can carry another horse back for Ty."

Jena's hand landed on her arm. "I'm really sorry about the mix-up. Harm didn't tell me he'd already given you permission to stay at my aunt's house."

"It's been a good way to avoid Chad." Evan gave them a sheepish smile.

"I've a mind to un-invite him to the wedding." Harm didn't bother to hide the annoyance in his tone.

Jena glanced at her fiancé. "You know your parents are best friends with the mayor and his wife. There's no reason to cause tension. I'm sure Chad had had a few beers tonight. He'll be fine at the wedding."

Evan nodded, relieved that Jena had jumped in to calm Harm's temper. "I agree. I don't want to cause any more friction."

Harm gave her a curt nod. "Fine. But if Chad so much as steps one foot out of line at my wedding, I'll personally kick his ass."

"I have no doubt you'll follow through, too," Evan replied with a chuckle. "Well, I'm heading out."

"Why don't you come to the rehearsal party tomorrow?" Jena suggested. "Since the wedding and the reception will be held outside at our ranch, to appease my mom's need for formality she's hosting a semiformal party at the Wilshire Hotel tomorrow night. If you can work it around your schedule, you're welcome to come."

"Are you sure? Isn't the party after the rehearsal typically for the wedding party?"

Jena laughed. "Usually, but my mom's invited the world to this affair, it seems."

Evan knew Ty would be there. The idea of spending an entire day with the irresistible man made her stomach flutter. "Count me in. Thanks for inviting me."

With each step she took across the wooden floor toward the bar's exit, Evan's excitement grew. Ty's words reverberated in her head, *I'll see you back at the Double D*.

* * * * *

The house was dark as she drove up the long drive. Disappointment filled her that she'd somehow missed Ty. That is until her car's lights landed on Ty leaning against the porch post...as if he were waiting for her.

Evan's heart raced and her stomach tensed. She'd been so confident when she'd told Ty she knew how to please herself, but would he find her inexperience with men a turnoff or lacking in some way?

She cut the engine and turned off the car's lights, dousing the house in darkness. After she'd shut her car door and started to approach the porch, she couldn't decide which was louder, the buzzing of night bugs or her own pulse racing in her ears.

Ty had his arms crossed over his chest in a casual stance. When she stood on the step below him, he didn't move or say a word. But even in the moon's light, she saw the glitter of desire in his gaze as he raked it down her body.

"I won't make you any promises."

"I don't expect any." Her lower stomach muscles tensed at his curt, dark tone.

"My way."

"Fine." She lifted her chin a notch at the challenge in his gaze. It was as if he were goading her, trying to get her to cry off.

"Come here," he commanded, his voice a low rumble.

Taking a deep breath, Evan climbed the final step and stood in front of him.

He didn't move, didn't lower his arms. He just stared at her with his intense gaze. Yet she felt his heat and her body reacted to his closeness…even with the wall of control and folded arms he held between them.

The tense silence lingering between them was getting to her. Evan started to speak, to break the tension, but Ty chose that moment to lower his arms and take a step toward her.

"What did he do to you?" he asked.

"What?" She took a step back.

"If Chad didn't have sex with you, how far did he get?" he grated out as he turned and took another step.

His action forced her to back toward the door if she wanted to keep her gaze locked with his. Why did she feel he was purposefully trying to rile her?

The toe of his boot landed between her feet on the floorboards. He crowded her personal space, his broad shoulders making her feel small for a woman of her height. Or was it his dominant charisma that made her feel that way? The tension emanating from him caused her to take another step back, but this time her boot heel hit the front door. Her heart raced while her stomach clenched at his question.

"I don't see what Chad and I did has any relevance."

The moon's light behind him immersed Ty's face in shadows. He placed a hand on the door behind her, caging her in.

"Did he touch you, bring you to climax with his hands?" he continued in a husky tone.

Evan's heart raced at his relentless, intimate questions.

When she didn't respond, Ty lowered his face close to hers. "It doesn't matter. For the next couple of days, I'm going to be the only man on your mind, the only man you want sliding inside you."

There was something about the quiet certainty of his tone that scared her. It wasn't arrogance on his part, but more an assured confidence that had her breath hitching in her throat. Could she handle what Ty was sure to throw her way?

"I'm going to push you to your limit, take you out of your comfort zone."

Her spine stiffened at his low threat. "How do you know I won't take you out of yours?"

White teeth flashed in the dark. She felt his feral smile like a tiger running his tongue along her shoulder, sampling his prey before he took his first, deep bite.

"You're welcome to try."

It was now or never. She had to show him she was no one's patsy to be pushed around.

Evan grasped his package through his jeans then ran her fingers over his erection before cupping his cock.

His body tensed and she heard his hissing intake of breath. She gave him a knowing smile. "I'm ready."

Ty reached down and pried her fingers off his erection. Lacing his hand with hers, he grasped her other hand and pulled them up over her head. He pressed her hands against the door behind her. "I said, my way."

Her heart galloped at the forceful warning in his tone. Did he think he was going to lead the entire time? She might be innocent in some ways, but she definitely had a mind of her own and she damned well planned to use it.

"Kiss me, damn it," she demanded.

Instead of kissing her mouth, Ty's lips grazed her jaw.

She gasped at the sensation of his five o'clock shadow rasping against her soft skin. When she tried to turn her mouth toward his, he moved his lips to her neck and nipped at her skin.

His hot breath bathed her neck as he kissed a trail to the hollow at the base of her throat. Evan moaned at the torture he seemed willing to put her though. "You're going in the wrong direction."

"Shhh," he said before he kissed her chin.

Ty's mouth felt warm and moist and so damn sexy. How could he expect her to just stand there and take it?

When he kissed the corner near her mouth, she tried once more to capture his mouth with hers, but he grasped her lower lip between his teeth and held her still.

Evan panted at his need to establish the pace between them. It made her want to push his buttons, to shove him over the edge.

She flicked her tongue out and traced it along his upper lip.

Ty's fingers tightened around hers right before his mouth covered hers. His tongue slid against hers in one of the hottest kisses she'd ever experienced. Heat flooded from her breasts all the way down to her center.

Evan tried to pull her hands free in order to wrap her arms around him, but a low growl rumbled in his chest as he held her still. Other than his hands, lips and tongue, no other part of his body touched hers.

And, ohmigod, what he could do with those sexy lips and that seductive tongue. He delved deep in slow, methodical thrusts, exploring her mouth, teasing her tongue, making her ache to feel him inside her just like that.

"Let me go. I want to touch you," she panted between kisses.

"No," Ty said before he pressed his mouth against hers, harder this time.

No? What the hell? Anger filled her and she bit down on his tongue, stopping their kiss. Releasing his tongue, she asked, "Aren't you going to touch me?"

Ty let go of her hands and took a step away with a tense look on his face.

"Tomorrow."

Tomorrow? Was he screwing with her mind? He was only here for a few more days. His tense shoulders and the rise and fall of his chest told her he wanted to go further.

She narrowed her gaze. "Are you teasing me?"

He shook his head. "No. I told you. We'll do this my way. You can back out at any time you want."

Evan clenched her jaw in frustration. The man was determined to draw this out. Suffering sexual frustration was not her idea of fun. She'd had enough of that on her own.

Grabbing the doorknob behind her, she opened the door and bit out, "Your loss."

Ty watched Evan stomp across the room and open and close her bedroom door. His balls ached like a motherfucker at the sight of her sweet ass swaying in her jeans. Every fiber in his body screamed at him to chase her down and rip her clothes off. To go at it like two wild rabbits, just like she wanted.

But Evan's virginity held him at bay. He wanted her so fucking turned on, she'd be prepared and begging for it when he took her. Slow and controlled was the best way to handle Evan…even if she didn't see it that way.

Ty lay down on the couch and adjusted his aching cock in his jeans. He groaned inwardly that he seemed to be in this perpetual mode of blue-ball arousal when it came to Evan. When he'd seen that jackass Chad demanding Evan's attention, something in him snapped. That had to explain his getting involved and his surprising decision to ignore his personal rule against sleeping with virgins. All he knew was sheer fury had swept through him. He'd had to work hard to concentrate on all he'd been taught in his aikido training. *Take deep breaths and remain calm. Use your opponent's anger and force against him.*

He'd wanted to snap the fucker's arm.

When the air-conditioning turned off, the house grew achingly quiet. If he'd followed Evan's request, the small ranch house would be full of the sounds and smells of heart-pounding sex. He closed his eyes at that thought and his cock turned unbelievably hard. Ty gritted his teeth and tried breathing techniques to calm his raging libido.

Once his pulse stopped pounding in his ears, the sound of feminine moans permeated his consciousness. Ty jerked his gaze toward the bedroom door to see it was ajar.

It must've popped open when the air-conditioning clicked off.

Another moan floated his way, this one deeper than the last. As if invisible, seductive fingers beckoned him, he stood and walked toward the door. He couldn't resist the arousing sound.

Ty paused outside her door then slowly pushed it wide open.

The sight before him shot a jolt of sheer stimulation straight to his cock.

The moon's light from the side window spread across the bed, illuminating Evan's gorgeous long legs. She was lying on her back, her neck and spine arched as she thrust her fingers deep inside her channel. The white tank top she wore only accentuated her dark nipples jutting against the thin cotton.

Ty's balls began to throb. He clenched his fists by his sides and fought the desire to join her—desire that raced through him in sparks of fiery arousal. If he didn't know better, he'd swear she did it on purpose just to throw him over the edge.

But Evan seemed completely oblivious to his presence and her uninhibited responses to her own stimuli only made him want her more. When she climaxed and sighed, Ty started to close the door to give her privacy.

But the door chose that moment to squeak. Fuck!

Evan gasped and her eyes flew open. She grabbed the sheet and pulled it over herself as she sat up on her elbow.

Ty straightened his spine and gave her an unapologetic look. "Now we're even." He shut the door quietly behind him.

Embarrassed heat stole up Evan's cheeks. She stared at the closed door while her heart jerked and her body still ached for a more fulfilling release. Not only had Ty just watched her get herself off, but from the comment he made, the man knew she'd witnessed him doing the same in the shower. As mortified as she was, a thought struck her—had he been as turned on as she was by the sight? She snorted in annoyance and lay down once more. Obviously not, since he'd walked away.

Pulling the covers up to her chin, she contemplated what it would take to get Ty to totally lose it. His control intrigued her, drew her in like a moth to a flame, but at the same time his steely persona infuriated her. All she wanted to do was jump his bones. She didn't want her first sexual experience to be on a timetable. She wanted it to be spontaneous and uninhibited and as real as it could be.

Chapter Four

Ty had been working nonstop since dawn. He was glad he'd worn his boots for the work Harm threw his way. The warm late-morning sun beat down on him, growing hotter by the minute. He'd ditched his shirt an hour earlier and sweat now coated his skin as he stopped the tractor he'd been driving and jumped down.

Granted, he'd worked his ass off this morning for a reason—named Evan...or Eve, he thought with a smirk. The woman was certainly the epitome of forbidden temptation, all wrapped up in a gorgeous five-foot-ten woman he wanted nothing more than to bury himself into. Last night was one of the longest nights of his life.

After today's chores he knew he'd ache all over, but work had always been his escape—that and aikido. Jena had looked at him differently this morning as if she were surprised to learn something about him she didn't know. He'd smiled in memory at the look he'd seen on Jena's face last night when he'd taken Chad down. He never did tell his kid sis about his martial arts abilities. For him, aikido was more than just a tool for keeping in shape. It helped him learn to focus, to get over past issues in his life and move on.

"Want me to help out in the stables?" Ty called out to Harm.

Harm pulled a cowboy hat off the hook on the wall in the stables and threw it to him. "Yeah, hitch the flatbed to the tractor and get Keith to help you load up a couple of bales of hay for the stables."

"Does that mean I'll be mucking, too?" Ty chuckled as he plunked the black Stetson on his head.

Harm flashed him a wide smile. "I knew I was marrying into a smart family."

Ty just shook his head. "Good thing I brought a change of clothes."

* * * * *

Evan's SUV bumped and jostled over the gravel road as she drove up to Steele Way ranch. She hoped Flash would be okay. Hell, the horse should feel very cozy. Evan had had to line the trailer with hay in order to get the skittish animal to go near it. Once she got Flash inside, the horse seemed to settle. Harm had said Flash loved going places, so maybe it'd been the double trailer that wigged the mare a bit. Evan wasn't certain of the reason, but she was glad disguising the trailer as a stall did the trick.

Jena met her as she jumped out of her vehicle. "Hi, Evan." Jena's gaze traveled from Evan's newly cutoff jeans and cropped T-shirt to her broken-in cowboy boots.

She grinned when her blue gaze met Evan's once more. "I had no idea your legs were so long. You should wear shorts more often."

Evan glanced down at her tan legs, thankful she'd worn shorts as much as she could when she was at home working in the yard. She laughed and moved around the back of the trailer to open the latch.

Three ranch hands rushed forth, saying in unison, "Here, let us help ya with that, Evan."

"Then again…" Jena began in an amused whisper as she followed her around the trailer, cowboys following behind, "I think you'll put a real dent in the amount of work the ranch hands will get done today."

As the three men shouldered their way past each other, trying to get the horse down, Evan chuckled. "Hmmm, maybe it's a good thing I only plan to be here for an hour to exercise Flash."

"You are coming to the rehearsal party tonight, right?" Jena asked.

Evan nodded. "I wouldn't miss it."

Grasping Flash's bridle, Evan met Jena's gaze. "I thought I saw Ty's car. Is he here?"

Despite Evan's casual tone, Jena gave her a knowing grin. "Yeah, Harm's working Ty's butt off." A thoughtful expression crossed her face. "Which is kind of interesting to see him working so hard because my brother has always hated Texas heat."

Evan glanced back at Jena as the woman followed her over to the gated area. "Really?"

Jena nodded. "Ty really doesn't like Texas. When we came here to sell off my aunt's property a couple of months ago, he couldn't wait to get back home." She tilted her head as she reminisced. "Come to think of it, he seemed to like visiting my aunt the couple of summers we spent with her." She sighed and flipped her blonde hair over her shoulder. "But then he'd grown up that last summer we spent here and I guess ranching bored him."

Evan opened a gate to a pasture. She'd just pulled the bridle off Flash when she heard a tractor over near the stables. "Go enjoy a nice jaunt, ole girl," she said, patting the horse's neck.

"Speak of the devil..." Jena said, drawing Evan's attention to her line of sight.

Evan's heart rammed in her chest at the sight before her. Ty's broad, muscular back was to her as he and another ranch hand rolled a bale of hay off the trailer next to the stables.

Ty happened to turn at that moment and his gaze locked with hers. Evan thought for sure her heart had stopped beating for a second or two...the man so effectively took her breath away.

His gloved hand touched the rim of his cowboy hat in acknowledgement while his gaze traveled to her exposed waist and legs before meeting hers once more. A slow, sexy smile formed on his lips making her stomach clench in anticipation.

Evan couldn't stop her own gaze from trailing over Ty's well-formed body. He had the perfect triangular shape. Broad shoulders and a trim waist. A thin line of dark hair started at his belly button and narrowed past his buckle into his jeans. Beyond his washboard stomach, his body was so fit he even had those mouthwatering defined muscles that dipped past the waistline of his jeans, splitting his lower belly and waist into three perfect sections of cut muscles. Her fingers itched to run along his chiseled physique, to feel the hard flesh flexing against her.

"It's a good thing my brother has been working his ass off, 'cause now he isn't going to get a bit of work done." Jena chuckled next to her.

Jena's comment jerked her out of her fantasy. "Don't worry, Jena, I won't keep Ty from working."

Jena grinned. "I was just teasing you, Evan. Ty's here for my wedding and a bit of vacation time, too. I would love to see him enjoy Texas again. Then maybe he'd visit me more than for my wedding."

Evan heard the sad tone in Jena's voice. She hoped Ty enjoyed his stay, too. That meant he might come back for a visit in the future. *Don't even go there, girl*, she thought to herself.

Evan watched as Ty turned and began to break apart the bale of hay. Her stomach knotted at the shoulder and back muscles that bunched with each move he took.

"Hmmm, then again, maybe you should come by the ranch more often. I've never seen the men so…motivated," Jena mused, glancing at the three ranch hands who were in the process of cleaning out the trailer's floor for Evan.

* * * * *

Ty threw himself into his work. Harm must've been yanking his chain because the stalls had already been mucked. Fortunately, all he had to do was fill them with fresh hay.

As he moved back to the broken bale, he and Evan met face to face, their pitchforks digging in at the same time.

"Hey," she said in a low, husky voice.

Ty's groin instantly hardened at the sight of her cheeks rosy from work. His gaze gravitated to the cleavage the vee in her T-shirt allowed as she bent to retrieve a forkful of hay for her trailer, then returned to her face. She'd pulled her hair back into a ponytail and ringlets had escaped the band to frame her face in light, sweaty curls.

He glanced at the trailer she'd been working to fill with fresh hay. "Need some help?"

She lifted the scoopful of hay and turned away, calling over her shoulder, "No thanks. I'm almost done."

Ty watched as she walked up the trailer's incline. When she dropped the hay and bent slightly to spread it with the pitchfork, he almost choked as swift arousal slammed into his gut.

Her cutoff shorts rode her cheeks, giving him a perfect view of her ass while making him want to see the small private area the denim barely covered. He had no idea why the sight of those boots at the bottom of her long legs turned him on, but damn...they did.

He swallowed and swiped his gloved hand across his sweaty brow. That's when he noticed several ranch hands had stopped working as if mesmerized. Some men were leaning against the fence, while others had paused mid-stride as they walked past.

When Evan leaned the pitchfork against the wall and dropped to her knees, preparing to spread the hay with her hands, biting jealousy gripped him. He knew the view the men were about to see. No fucking way were they getting that kind of show. Ty narrowed his gaze on the men. "Is it lunchtime yet?"

His curt comment snapped the men back to attention. With one last glance Evan's way, the men turned back to their work.

Ty grabbed his discarded shirt and shrugged into it as his boots ate up the distance between Evan and him. He mounted the metal ramp, ready to lay into her, but the sight of her sweet ass swaying as she moved around on her hands and knees caused the words to lodge in his throat.

Very little light filtered into the trailer. The roof and sides made the space feel hot and secluded as he moved deeper into the room. He didn't care if it smelled of horses. It was his own private haven with the woman who'd managed to haunt his sleep.

The bits of hay Evan had dropped on her way up the ramp must've muffled his approach because Evan apparently hadn't heard him coming. She continued moving around, spreading the hay with quick actions, oblivious to his presence. The lecherous part of him didn't want to end the show either now that his body blocked anyone else's view.

His heart rammed in his chest and his erection rubbed uncomfortably against his jeans. He adjusted his cock, trying to relieve the pressure his zipper caused. Touching himself only managed to turn him on more. Ty gritted his teeth, holding back his baser instincts to lean over and touch Evan. He could so easily slip his fingers past the tiny crotch of her jeans into her wet heat underneath.

He heard her heavy breathing as she worked and couldn't help imagining her breathing like that for an entirely different reason. He wanted her like this, breathless and sweaty, bent over and ready to take him.

He closed his eyes, fighting his desire. But when he opened them and Evan actually wiggled her nicely rounded ass as she began to back up, he lost the battle.

Ty narrowed his gaze and squatted. With deliberate determination, he pulled the gloves off his hands and tossed them to the floor. Resting his forearms on his knees, he sat and waited for Evan to back into him.

His cock ached when she was within two feet. She'd stopped to grab something underneath the hay. Ty's patience had snapped. He started to move forward, to clasp her curved hips, when something hard hit him on the forehead.

Pain radiated up his head. "Sonofabitch!" he hissed as he fell onto his back and grabbed his brow right above his right eye.

"Ohmigod, Ty!" Evan leaned over him and grabbed his hand. "I'm so sorry. I didn't know you were behind me."

"Apparently not," he said in a dry tone as he pulled his hand away from his head. Bright red blood covered his palm. "What'd you hit me with? A shovel?"

Evan's brow furrowed as she looked at his cut. "No, Flash's bridle had fallen from the wall where I'd hung it earlier. It was underneath the hay. I was tossing it behind me to get it out of the way..." She paused and a perplexed look crossed her face. "Though I have no idea how I threw it so high it hit you in the forehead."

"I can think of better ways to get me flat on my back."

She rolled her eyes at his blatant, sexy comment as she grabbed his hand and started to pull him to his feet. "Come on. I have a feeling that cut needs stitches."

Ty shrugged off the pain and stood on his own. "Nah, I'll be fine."

A stubborn look crossed Evan's face. "You're going to the doctor even if I have to hogtie you again to get you there. Put your hand on your cut until I can get a bandage for you," she ordered before she ran down the ramp and disappeared.

Ty sighed and did as she asked as he exited the trailer.

Evan met him as he came around the side of her SUV. "Okay, let me see it."

He lowered his hand once more and she placed a bandage over his cut.

"Ow!" He winced and tried to pull back from the stinging pain.

She grabbed his arm and held him still while she applied pressure. "Stop being a baby. That's an antiseptic to disinfect your cut. Keep it on there while I drive you to the doctor."

Jena walked out of her house and ran down the steps once she saw Ty holding a bandage to his head. "What happened?"

"I, uh, whacked your brother with Flash's bridle by accident. Since the trailer's hooked to my SUV, can I borrow your truck to take him to Dr. Shelton's office?"

"Yes, of course." Jena glanced at her brother as she clasped his arm. "Are you okay?"

Ty rolled his eyes then winced at the pain. "I'm fine. I don't need to go to the doctor, you two."

A stubborn expression crossed Jena's face. "If Evan says you need to see a doctor, then you will go."

"She's just overreacting." Ty felt the women were definitely going overboard.

"Evan's a—"

"Um, we'd better get going," Evan quickly said, interrupting his sister.

"Yes, no point in arguing with him," Jena agreed. "I'll be right back with my keys."

When Jena returned with the keys, she said, "I'm going, too."

Ty shook his head "No, you're not. You have more important things to do. Like get ready for your rehearsal."

"Are you sure?" Indecision reflected in his sister's gaze.

Evan took the keys. "Positive. Ty's in good hands."

Jena cast a thankful gaze Evan's way. "I know that for a fact. Thanks, Evan."

Once they'd climbed in Jena's vehicle, Evan drove straight to Dr. Shelton's office.

Ty's Temptation

Ty cast his gaze her way and noted her stiff posture as she pressed harder on the gas pedal. "Slow down, speedy. It's not like I'm in danger of passing out on you."

"It's ten 'til twelve. Dr. Shelton closes at noon on Fridays."

Ty studied her. Yeah, they were short on time, but something else was bothering her. A few seconds ago she was concerned, but she still joked and reprimanded him. Now she seemed tense. What had caused her change of mood?

* * * * *

Ty walked into Dr. Shelton's office behind Evan. While he filled out the paperwork, the doctor's secretary said, "Hi, Evan. It's good to see you. If you two will have a seat, Dr. Shelton will be out in a minute."

Ty and Evan had been sitting all of a minute when a side door opened and a dark-haired woman in a long white physician's coat walked out.

"Ty Hudson. I can't believe it!" She looked up from her clipboard. Her surprised brown gaze locked with his.

Ty's chest constricted. He stood and worked hard not to show any emotion as he responded in a low tone, "Lily. It's been a long time."

Evan stood beside him. She glanced at him in curiosity before addressing the doctor. "Hi, Lily. Ty needs stitches and probably a tetanus shot, too."

"Come on back." Lily smiled at him.

Ty's stomach knotted as he started to take a step to follow her back to the exam room. Lily stopped when Evan joined him.

"You can wait out here, Evan. I can take it from here."

Ty glanced at Evan and noted the determined set of her lips. He could tell she was about to insist on coming back with them. "I'll be fine. Be right back," he said.

The hurt look on her face pulled at his heart, but Ty didn't want Evan to hear the mini-version of his past he was sure Lily would dredge up. Hell, he didn't want to hear it either.

Once Evan walked back to sit down, Ty followed Lily through a door, past a couple of doors until they reached an empty exam room. His gaze ate up her petite, trim figure and her pitch-black hair clamped in a quick twist. She'd grown into the beautiful, sophisticated woman he'd always thought she would become.

Lily closed the exam room door behind them. "Since I'll be working on your forehead, have a seat on the stool. When'd you last have a tetanus shot?"

"Six months ago."

She nodded and jotted down a note on his chart. "Since your last tetanus shot was so recent, I think you'll be fine without one."

Ty sat down on the cushioned rolling stool and waited.

"I couldn't believe it when I read the name on the patient's form." Lily washed and dried her hands then retrieved a bottle of antiseptic and cotton balls from the white, glass-doored cabinet.

"Yeah, a real shocker," he commented. Floored was more like it. The last thing he expected was for the town's doctor to be the woman he'd fallen in love with all those years ago. "I see you married." He glanced at her name badge. Her familiar jasmine scent invaded his senses. At least one thing about her hadn't changed.

"Soon to be divorced." A smirk curved her lips as she moved closer while pulling on a pair of rubber gloves.

Now that comment surprised him. He started to raise his eyebrow but winced at the pain his action caused.

"Hold still." Lily dabbed at his wound above his eyebrow with a cotton ball. Ty closed his eyes, blocking his view of her breasts, exposed by her v-neck cotton shirt under her open jacket. Once she'd cleaned the wound thoroughly, he felt her fingers manipulating his skin. "You have a nasty cut. Evan's right. You need stitches. Do you want a painkiller?"

Ty met her gaze and shook his head. He wanted to remember the pain this woman caused him. Having her inflict him with more would be a perfect physical reminder.

"How'd this happen?" she asked before returning to the cabinet.

"Got hit with a flying bridle." Ty watched her prepare the needle and thread.

Lily raised a perfectly arched eyebrow and cast an amused gaze his way. "That's not something one hears every day." She turned away from the counter and approached him holding a scissors-type instrument. The end of the instrument was pinched closed, holding the needle and thread.

"I expected you to leave Boone. To seek that 'better life' you wanted." The comment came out before he could stop it. Why did he torture himself? he wondered.

She met his gaze with her steady chocolate brown one before she grasped his jaw and turned his head to the side so she could see better. "I got married. To a surgeon, no less."

"Not surprised," he grated out at the same time the needle pierced his skin above his eyebrow. Son of a bitch! That hurt. Ty forced himself to ignore the stinging pain.

She pursed her lips at his sarcastic jibe and continued to suture his wound. "Life doesn't always turn out as one plans. So what do you do now?"

Her tone might be conversational, but he felt the slight tug on the thread. No fucking way was he telling her he was a very successful architect. "A little of this and a little of that."

She chuckled at his vague response. "When I read Harm's wedding announcement in the paper and saw he was marrying your sister, I hoped you'd come back to Boone." Lily tied a knot and snipped the thread.

"Oh?" he asked, surprised by her statement.

Even though she'd finished her task, Lily hadn't moved out of his personal space.

"I never forgot about you."

Was that interest he heard in her voice? Ty's gut clenched.

He heard his own pulse rushing in his ears while Lily's words, spoken over two decades ago, came rushing back.

"Marry you? I don't want to be hemmed in by marriage. I want to make something of myself, Ty. To be someone important." He heard her voice as if it were yesterday. Each word had stabbed at his heart, shattering his image of true love. He'd loved her, damn it.

"You didn't want me back then," he reminded her in a cold tone.

Lily placed her hands on his cheeks. "We were seventeen, Ty. Too young to know what we wanted out of life."

"And did you find it?" he challenged, angrier then he'd ever been in his life.

Her gaze searched his as she moved her mouth closer to his. "Yeah, I think I just did."

Before her lips could connect, Ty grabbed her wrists and set her away from him. He released her and stood up from the stool. "Thank you for closing my wound." He was very aware of the irony of his words. While she'd just mended one wound, she ripped open another—one that took a helluva lot more than stitches to close.

Seeing Lily again made him relive the devastating hurt she'd caused him all those years ago. Churning emotions he'd long buried, surfaced anew, tearing at his gut, making his stomach burn.

"Congratulations on the professional life you've created for yourself, Lily. I'm happy for you," he said before he opened the door and walked out.

"Let's go," Ty snarled as he walked out of the doctor's office.

Evan rushed to keep up with his long, determined strides. What was going on? Why did he seem angry? And here she thought she was the one all wound up.

Evan had been so tense waiting for Lily to take care of Ty's wound. While it was true she could've stitched his wound herself, the truth was she really didn't want to have to take him to her office. The name Evan Masters, DVM, plastered on her veterinary office's front door was a dead giveaway. She wasn't quite ready to share that part of herself with Ty. Not yet. Maybe never, since he'd be leaving in a few days anyway.

"Lily got you all fixed up?" Evan asked, trying to lighten his mood.

"You could say that." He put his hand out for the keys. "I'll drive."

Evan met his deep green gaze, hoping to see some emotion, something to give her a clue as to his current mood. He stared at her with an inscrutable expression.

Her gaze moved to the stitches above his brow line as she dropped the keys in his hand. "I'm really sorry."

"No big deal." He wrapped his fingers around the keys and opened the passenger side door for her.

She climbed inside and waited for Ty to come around to his side and slide into his seat. They'd driven for a few minutes in silence when Ty finally spoke.

"I don't think we're such a good idea."

"What'd you say?" she asked, her heart tightening.

Ty kept his gaze on the road. "I think it's best if we keep it platonic between us. Chad knows you're staying with me. That should be enough to keep him at bay."

His words hurt her more than they should've. She felt like someone had just grabbed her heart with both hands and twisted each half in opposite directions. Why did she have a feeling his change of heart had to do with Lily? Evan might not have been socially aggressive growing up—hell, she was at least two years and in some cases, three years younger than her classmates in college and vet and business school—but she'd never been one to hold back when she felt the need to speak her mind. And she wasn't about to start now.

"You're chicken."

"What the hell did you just say?" He cut his gaze her way, green eyes sparking in anger.

She crossed her arms over her chest. "You heard me. Bock, bock. What are you afraid of, Ty? That you might like it a little too much?"

Ty's jaw clenched. "You're awfully smug for a virgin."

She ignored his jab. "I didn't take you for the fowl type."

"I'll be gone day after tomorrow."

"All the more reason not to worry you'll get too attached," she challenged, meeting his narrowed gaze head-on.

"The deal's off." He turned his gaze back to the road and tightened his fingers on the steering wheel.

We'll see about that. She turned away to stare out the window while sheer determination simmered inside her.

When they drove up Steele Way's main drive, Jena came out of the stables wiping her hands on her jeans. "How's your head?" she greeted her brother as he and Evan got out of her truck.

Ty dropped the truck's keys in her hand. "I'm as good as new." He didn't say a word to Evan before he walked off toward the stables.

As Evan came around the front side of the truck, Jena asked, "What caused that surly mood?"

Evan shrugged. "I was hoping you could tell me. Didn't you say you and your brother spent a couple summers here when you were younger?"

Jena nodded.

"Do you know if Ty and Lily Shelton knew each other back then?"

Jena's brow furrowed for a second. "Oh yeah. That Lily. Her married last name threw me. I'd forgotten about Ty dating Lily. The last summer he came to Texas, he and Lily spent a lot of time together. I hardly saw my brother those couple of months. That's why I ended up hanging with my cousins." She smiled. "The Tanner boys kept me busy dodging their teasing ways."

Evan's heart constricted at the news, but discovering Ty and Lily had a past explained his mercurial change of mood. "Were they serious then?"

Jena eyed her and a small smile formed on her lips. "Ah, I see where this is going."

Evan's stomach tensed. She needed to lighten Jena's serious thoughts. "You do? If so, I'd like to be in on the secret. Your brother will be gone in two days, Jena. I have no expectations other than to enjoy his company while he's here. His mood went in the tank once he saw Lily."

As soon as Evan spoke, a sudden sinking realization hit her. Maybe the reason Ty called it off with her was because he wanted to rekindle an old flame with Lily while he was here. The thought made her stomach cramp into tight, hard knots. She sighed as her own good spirits dropped considerably.

Jena put her hand on Evan's shoulder. "I don't know what to say, Evan. My brother has always been pretty quiet when it comes to his relationships. He's not one to share much." A sympathetic look crossed her face. "Are you still going to come to the rehearsal party this evening?"

Evan straightened her spine. She'd gone this long without a guy. There was no reason to be concerned about a man she never had in the first place. "Absolutely. I'll be there…and I'll even wear a dress."

Jena smiled. "That's the spirit!"

Evan's gaze strayed to Ty as he came walking out of the stables with a bag of grain across his shoulders. He'd taken his shirt off again. The play of muscles across his chest made her mouth water before he turned to head to the back of the building. Damn, the man was built.

Evan let out the breath she'd been holding. "Well, I'd better collect Flash and a mount for Ty and then I'll head back. Tell Harm I'll keep Flash until the wedding is over. She should be back to her old self by then."

Jena smiled her appreciation. "Harm will be relieved to have her back. He doesn't like me riding the other horses as much. Says he trusts Flash's genteel nature when it comes to me."

"It's so obvious when he looks at you that Harm is very much in love."

Jena gave a soft laugh. "I love him very much, too."

The adoration reflected in Jena's gaze as she looked at her fiancé across the yard, solidified Evan's personal vow. No matter how long it took, no matter how old she was…she refused to fall in love with a man who couldn't give her all his love in return.

Chapter Five

Evan drove up to the small house she shared with Ty, her emotions churning. After she'd loaded up the horses and taken them to the Double D, she'd spent the last couple of hours at her office seeing clients who'd begged to be squeezed in on her "vacation" day. She didn't mind. Work was distracting, which helped her forget about Ty for a while. But as she parked her vehicle next to Ty's rental car, she couldn't help the tightening of her stomach or the way her breathing hitched at the idea of seeing the man again.

Her stomach rumbled, reminding her it was way past lunchtime. The last thing she ate was a bagel for breakfast. But the sensation of her heart hammering as she opened her car door and closed it behind her, overshadowed her need for food. She started toward the house when she heard one of the horses neighing in the stables.

Leaving her backpack beside her car's tire, Evan walked over to the stables. As she entered the small building, the sight of Ty grooming his horse made her pulse race. He faced away from her, giving her an oh-so perfect view of just how well his jeans hugged his nice ass.

The well-worn material cupped his cheeks and muscular thighs in such an inviting way, she wanted to walk up and run her hands down the soft material. She knew the contrast of worn denim covering hard muscles would turn her on like no other. Or was it his broad, naked back she wanted to press herself against that got her motor going?

Why not? she told herself as she approached him from behind. He may like soft, petite women like Lily, but Evan could show him what it was like to hold a woman who wasn't afraid to get her nails dirty.

When she was a step away, Ty paused his movements, holding the brush an inch above the horse's back.

He didn't turn to acknowledge her, but she knew he was aware of her presence.

His back tensed when she ran her fingers across his shoulder blades. Was that a rejection? She bit her lip and her stomach knotted. Her entire body stiffened, ready for his brush-off.

Evan almost pulled her hands away, but the play of tight muscles under her fingers was just too irresistible. Instead she moved her hands lower to cup those sexy defined muscles that ran around the front of his waist.

When she pressed her body against his back and started to move one of her hands toward his pectoral, Ty grabbed her wrist. "Evan—"

"Let me touch you." She planted a kiss on his warm skin.

Ty's grip on her hand tightened for a second then loosened. He moved both his hands to the horse's back, allowing her to continue her exploration.

Evan's fingers flexed across his hard pectoral. The thick muscle jumped under her fingers, making her smile. Despite his reservations, he enjoyed her touch.

She let go of Ty and quickly ducked underneath his arms until she stood between the horse and him, facing Ty. The long, thick bulge pressed against the fly of his jeans made her heart race. Her gaze locked with his forest green one. They stood there, staring at one another for several long seconds. Her heart pounded at the intense look on his face and his clenched jaw.

Taking a steadying breath, she curled her fingers around his triceps then ran her palms up his shoulders. She stepped closer and moved her hands underneath his arms to trail her hands down his broad back. Evan thrilled at the heat emanating from him. She laid her cheek against his neck then kissed his tense jaw.

"I have no expectations, Ty. I know you'll be gone in a couple of days."

Ty didn't speak. Nor did he move to touch her. Frustration filled her at his stoic stance. His body told her he wanted. Maybe she just needed to show him how much.

She kissed the pulse beating a rapid throb at his throat while her fingers moved to the button on his jeans.

Ty let out a harsh breath at the same time he turned his head and trapped her face against his throat with his stubbled jaw. It was as if he couldn't help himself. Her heart skipped a beat when she heard him inhale as if drinking in her scent in one long gulp of air. The thought made her stomach flip-flop and her sex begin to throb.

He smelled so incredibly good, musky and spicy...of sandalwood, leather and sweat. She wanted to wallow in his scent, spread it all over her.

They stood in the shade, but the afternoon sun slanted across the horse's back. Bits of hay, probably stirred up from Ty bringing the horse back from a ride, floated in the warm air around them. As Evan pulled the buttons of his pants' fly apart, Ty purposely brushed his erection against her fingers.

Evan cupped his hard flesh through his fitted black cotton boxer briefs and the denim that still partially covered him. The man's impressive size made her sex flood with moisture.

She slid her hand inside his underwear and gripped the soft silky skin around his erection. Rubbing her thumb across the tip of his cock, she stood on tiptoe and pressed her chest against his, whispering in his ear. "I don't know what made you change your mind, but are you sure you really want to?"

Before he could respond, Evan went back down on her heels at the same time she hooked her fingers in the waist of his jeans and jerked, pulling his pants down to his thighs. His muscular thighs stopped the jeans' descent any farther than his buttocks, but she'd achieved her goal. His erection sprang free. Her heart raced at the erotic sight of his cock standing at rigid attention. She wanted to touch every single well-defined vein that lined his erection.

Ty grabbed her wrist before she could touch him.

Evan's eyes flashed in anger. She was ready to argue, when Ty took her hand and cupped it around his cock.

Her heart leapt at his action. She elevated her gaze to Ty's heated one as he squeezed her fingers tight around him. His grip was so firm, she not only felt every crease and vein, but when he slid her hand down his cock, she felt his steady heartbeat thumping.

"I feel your heartbeat." She didn't bother to hide the awe in her voice.

When he released her hand and refused to respond, she squeezed and used her hold to yank him closer. Damn the man and his controlled emotions!

Ty grunted when their bodies collided. The only sign she'd gotten to him was the slight flare of his nostrils. She wanted him involved and breathing hard. The man had yet to touch her. She knew he wanted her. Damn him.

She turned sideways and kissed a path down his muscular chest and abs. As her mouth moved toward his cock, she hoped to elicit some kind of reaction.

Ty grabbed her ponytail, stopping her descent.

Frustration mounted within her. The man blocked her every move. Evan's lips were a breath away from his erection. She was determined to win this round. Cupping his sac with her free hand, she blew her heated breath across the plum tip in one long tantalizing breath.

Ty's hips jerked forward at the same time she heard a low groan rumble in his chest.

He released her ponytail and Evan took advantage of her freedom. She encircled his erection with her lips, plunging his cock deep into the recesses of her mouth.

Ty's breathing changed as she began to slide her wet lips up and down the hard flesh. She sucked hard, locking her lips around him.

He speared his fingers in her bound hair, gripping the back of her head. Evan's heart raced when a low, ragged breath escaped his lips.

She ran her tongue in a slow, moist, decadent caress around his length like the red stripe that winds its way up a peppermint stick.

Ty's erection grew even harder in her mouth. He had to be close. Following her instincts, Evan began to suck hard, ready to take him over the edge. But Ty grabbed her shoulders and pulled her off him.

"Why—" she started to ask, but he cut her off, a steely, determined look on his face.

"My terms."

Her heart leapt at his comment. It meant he at least agreed to stick with their deal, but Evan narrowed her gaze at the fact he still wanted to dictate the how and when of it.

She shrugged out of his hold, determined to have the last word. A knowing smile crossed her face and she turned to walk away, saying, "I'm a helluva lot tighter than my mouth."

Before she'd taken one step, Ty grabbed her arm and yanked her close so his mouth rested against her temple.

"And I can guarantee I'll feel a helluva lot bigger than your three fingers."

Heat infused Evan's cheeks at his husky, blatantly intimate comment. It had the desired effect. His promise both scared and excited her. Her thighs trembled when he released her arm. She held her head high and forced one foot in front of the other as she walked out of the stables on unsteady legs.

Evan entered the cool house wanting to scream her frustration at the stubborn man. She definitely needed a shower to wash away a long day of work—a cold one would probably be best. With a heavy sigh, she headed for the bedroom, gathered a change of clothes then walked into the bathroom. Once she'd turned the faucet on, she pulled her shirt off and leaned over to place her hand under the hard, pulsing water. It was almost the right temperature. Hot. Oh, yeah…she needed a cold one. She started to turn the faucet to cold when someone's hand came around her waist.

Evan let out a scream as Ty pulled her naked back against his bare chest. Without a word, he leaned over and shut off the shower.

Evan's hands shook as she laid them over Ty's hand around her waist. The sudden quiet in the room made her nerves tighten while she stood there half naked in his embrace. Her stomach tensed and her heart raced as she wondered what he had planned.

Before she could turn to face him, Ty scooped her up in his arms and carried her out of the bathroom. Evan's hands landed on his broad, muscular shoulders as she gazed up at him.

Ty wasn't looking at her. His gaze was focused on the bed as he approached it. His boot heels ate up the low-pile, tan carpet in swift, determined strides.

When he set her down next to the bed, but kept one arm around her waist, she didn't know how she felt about the realization he'd yet to speak to her.

Despite the fact Evan stood in front of him only wearing her cutoff shorts and boots, she fought the red color she knew spread across her face. Straightening her shoulders, she refused to be embarrassed. She'd asked the man for so much more than standing there half naked in front of him. Glancing up at him, she was surprised to see how dark his green eyes had turned. His jaw ticced as he stared at her bare chest.

"Ty—"

His gaze collided with hers. "My way, Evan. Got it?"

An unspoken battle of wills seemed to stretch between them. She lowered her gaze to his chest and gritted her teeth at his stubborn stance.

Before she could ask him why, Ty's fingers slid up her neck until he touched her jaw. She shivered at the intimate contact.

He applied pressure so she had to meet his gaze. Heated arousal reflected in his serious stare.

"Understand?"

His softer tone and the look of sheer desire in his gaze melted her stubborn resolve to remain on equal footing. For now.

She started to nod, but his mouth covered hers, stopping her movement. His lips were warm, soft and so very persuasive. She opened her mouth and welcomed the slow, sensual glide of his tongue alongside hers.

Evan put her hands around his neck and started to step closer, but Ty cupped her breasts, his fingers gripping the mounds' soft tissue. Did he do that on purpose to keep her at a distance? When she tried to pull him closer, Ty slid his fingers to her nipples and rolled the tips between his thumb and index finger.

Pleasure radiated from her breasts and jolted straight down to her sex. Evan's heart raced as her fingers dug into the flesh on his shoulders.

Ty broke their kiss and let go of her. "Take off the rest of your clothes and lie down."

"What?" His commanding tone surprised her.

His steady gaze held hers. "You heard me."

Evan straightened her spine. "I don't take orders—"

"It wasn't an order. It was a request."

Evan bit her lower lip. Why was she fighting him so? She'd said she wanted this.

When she met his inscrutable gaze, she realized why. She wanted Ty to be just as involved, just as caught up. She wanted to shake that impenetrable control he'd built around himself.

As seconds ticked by, she glanced down to see his hands balled into fists by his sides as well as the huge bulge in the fly of his pants. The man wanted.

Now it was her job to make him want it more.

With a determined tilt of her chin, she locked her gaze with his as she kicked off her boots and unbuttoned her shorts. She shimmied out of her shorts and underwear with a purposeful jiggle of her breasts before she pulled off her socks with a sexy grin.

Her confidence faltered when she realized Ty's expression hadn't changed at her naked state. Disappointment settled in when she pulled the covers back and lay down on the bed.

Ty's gaze flicked toward the top of the bed. "Lean your back against the headboard."

Intrigued by his plan, Evan's pulse raced as she scooted up to the top of the bed. She shivered when her back met the cool wood of the tall headboard.

Ty pushed the covers to the bottom of the bed. Evan's gaze skimmed over his broad back as he sat down on the edge of the mattress and pulled his boots off. Instead of dropping his shoes, he set the boots beside the bed as if purposefully taking his time. Every move he made seemed precise and controlled. As exciting as his actions were, she wanted nothing more than to see what he'd be like if he was pushed too far.

Ty took a pillow and stuffed it behind her back, then turned on the bed and faced her. Her heart raced as he placed his hands on either side of her legs. "Bend your knees."

Bend her knees? But that would expose her completely. No way. She wanted to be on equal footing with him.

"Take off your clothes," she countered.

Her expression must've given him a clue as to her thoughts because he shook his head and continued in an even tone. "If you want this, you must completely let go of your inhibitions."

"What I want requires you to be just as naked as me," she shot back.

Ty raised his eyebrow in a deliberate challenge. "My—"

"I know, I know." Evan took a deep, steadying breath and bent her knees. When she started to place her feet flat on the bed against her body, Ty climbed on the bed and captured her heels.

Her stomach fluttered and her sex ached when he placed his knees on the outside of each of her thighs, then settled his rear on his calves before he lowered her feet to the bed on either side of this thighs.

Now her body truly surrounded his. If she thought the position he suggested before would expose her, this position allowed no privacy whatsoever.

Ty leaned forward and slid the rubber band out of her hair. His gaze remained fixed on her hair as he ran his fingers through the curls.

Once he'd tossed the rubber band to the floor, he leaned forward and his hands covered hers on the bed. Evan held back her gasp of excitement when he placed a kiss against her neck. While Ty leaned close, she took a deep breath. Leather, musk and a faint soap smell. If she tasted his skin, would he taste salty from the day's sweaty activities? She had to know.

Evan ran her tongue along his shoulder. She was surprised when she felt Ty shudder.

He pulled back. His green eyes narrowed. "My way, Evan."

He was salty...in more ways than one, yet he was still sexy as hell. "But—"

His hands tightened around hers.

"Are you saying I can't touch you?" she asked, incredulous.

"Not yet."

She let out an exasperated breath. "I just don't get you. How are we supposed to—"

Ty's mouth covered hers, cutting off her words. As his tongue thrust deep, tangling with hers, Evan's mind turned to mush. How was she supposed to argue with him when he was constantly distracting her with his seductive kisses?

She pressed her lips against his, countering his aggressive kiss with her own. God, could the man kiss. The act of his lips slanting over hers while his tongue invaded and enticed her active response sent pinpoints of excitement scattering throughout her body. She dug her toes in the bed and wished he'd let her hands go so she could explore his gorgeous body with more than just her eyes.

Ty moved his mouth to her ear. "Keep your hands right here."

"If I move my hands?" she challenged.

His serious green gaze met hers as he trailed his fingers across her shoulders in a light caress. "You won't get what you want."

Evan set her lips in a firm line and fisted her hands on the bed.

Ty's lips quirked upward as if he knew just how much of a battle it was for her to keep her hands still. His fingers slid over her collarbone then dropped lower until they cupped the edges of her breasts. Evan's stomach tensed when he spoke. "You said you know your own body, but do you really?"

The pads of his fingers skimmed her sensitive skin until they came close to her nipples.

Her breathing increased and she noted his raised eyebrow as if he expected her to respond to his question. The stitches above his other eyebrow only made him appear even more dark and intense.

"Yes."

He plucked at her nipples then pinched them. "Do you touch your breasts while you're getting off?"

She shrugged and fought the desire slamming through her at his touch. "Not really."

He shook his head then twirled her nipples before he pinched the tips once more. "That's a shame. Every part of your body, if stimulated properly, can elicit a sexual response."

Well, he had her on the nipple thing. Her sex reacted instantly to his stimulation, throbbing in aching need. As far as she was concerned there was only one other place on her body that responded to touch in a sexual sense.

He raised an eyebrow at her silence. "You don't believe me?"

She skimmed her gaze down his cut chest and six-pack abs to the bulge in his pants. "I know what part of my body responds to sexual stimulation."

Ty set his jaw at her comment. Now why had that angered him? When he moved his hands to her arms once more she wanted to wail.

He rubbed his fingers along her muscles then skimmed the pads down the skin along the inside of her arms. Evan shuddered at his touch. She had no idea that skin could be so sensitive.

Ty ran his hands back up her arms then pressed his palms against the sides of her breasts as he cupped his fingers around her sides. His hands began to move in slow, circular motions down her sides until he reached her waist.

Evan dug her short nails into her hands to keep from grabbing the man and pulling him against her. The sexy look in his eyes told her he knew what he was doing to her. He gripped her waist and ran his thumbs over her belly button.

Her lower belly moved in and out with her rapid breathing, while her insides pitched and fluttered in tense anticipation.

When he slid his index fingers between the crease where her legs met her body, Evan thought she was going to climax from the built-up anticipation. Her juices flooded in her channel and she throbbed in unfulfilled sexual desire.

Ty glanced down at her sex and smiled. "You're wet."

"That means I'm ready."

He shook his head at her snappy comment. "Not yet."

"Touch me, Ty," she begged.

"I am." His fingers continued their descent down the side of her sex, yet he didn't touch her.

Her stomach had begun to knot. She clamped her knees as close together as she could and panted out, "I can't take this."

Ty's serious gaze snapped to hers as he pulled her legs apart. "Yes, you can. I want to show you just how explosive it can be, Evan, not the quick orgasms you're used to experiencing, but a long satisfying one. You have to trust me."

"Right now I want to kill you," she bit out between clenched teeth.

He ignored her anger and focused his gaze on her sex once more.

She moaned and rocked her hips when his fingers touched her outer labia. But Ty didn't just briefly touch her. He rubbed the sensitive skin slowly between his fingers as if he were touching the softest of flower petals. Evan bit back her moan when his fingers moved to the inside of her labia where the tips of his fingers explored up and down the pink skin before he spread her wide open.

Evan gritted her teeth and closed her eyes at the sweet torture. If he didn't touch her soon, she was going to be arrested for committing murder. She could see her dad's shocked expression now. *"You killed him for delaying your orgasm?"*

"Open your eyes."

Evan's eyes snapped open at his husky tone. She glanced down at the pulse on his throat and managed a smile upon seeing its rapid pace. Good, she wasn't the only one affected.

Ty's finger ran along the inside edge of her entrance once more before he circled all the way around.

Evan bucked and whimpered, shutting her eyes.

"Look at me," he commanded. Evan's gaze locked with his. She sobbed when he slid a finger deep inside her. Her hips moved forward, ready to take all of him.

"Damn, you're tight and sopping wet," he gritted out.

Ty's Temptation

"I told—" She cut herself off and moaned in sheer pleasure when her skin seemed to stretch even more. He must've added another finger.

Ty began to thrust his fingers in and out of her body. When she moaned, he said, "You know I'm bigger than this, baby...a lot bigger."

She heard the warning in his tone and rocked her hips in earnest, seeking relief. "I'm looking forward to it."

His gaze lowered to his hand between them. He seemed enthralled by the sight.

Evan's breathing turned rampant as she lifted her hips to meet each of his thrusts. She was so close.

Ty's movements slowed and he withdrew his fingers to run them along the sensitive skin around her entrance. Now he was touching her inner labia.

"Wh-why did you stop?" She gripped the sheet tight in her fists and her breath hitched when he circled his finger around her clitoris.

Ty's steady gaze met hers as he slid his fingers inside her once more. Evan jerked her hips against him and relished the sensation of his fingers turning inside her, touching her thoroughly, intimately and oh-so purposefully. He was methodical, touching every section of her channel before pressing on a wonderful spot deep inside.

Evan felt her orgasm approaching. She closed her eyes and tensed her body, ready to welcome the passionate tremors.

Ty started to withdraw his hand once more. Her eyes jerked open and she grabbed his wrist, holding him close to her. "No!"

His gaze darkened and his expression turned hard. His fingers stilled inside her. "Do you want this? Want to come so bad you can't stand it?"

When she bit her lip and nodded, he skimmed his fingers across her hot-spot once more in a deliberate caress. "Then trust me."

She released his hand and let out an unsteady, sexually frustrated breath.

Ty watched the myriad expressions filter across Evan's face—frustration, fear, anger then reluctant acceptance.

Curls of strawberry-blonde hair stuck to the side of her face. Her cheeks were flushed and her skin literally glowed from her exertions. He'd always thought redheads were hot, but he came to the conclusion that a touch of red in blonde hair made him ache. Evan was so damn sexy, so sincere and natural in her responses…he'd never wanted a woman more than he did this one. She held nothing back. He saw every glimmer of emotion scatter across her face as she experienced them. It was the most erotic sex he'd ever had with a woman and he'd yet to slide inside her.

She began to whimper and roll her hips as he brushed her G-spot over and over again. Primal male satisfaction rose within him. He wanted to beat his chest—damn, he wanted to fuck her so bad he was sure he'd have blue balls before this session was over.

But he was determined to make this an experience Evan would never forget. To show her how satisfying her orgasm could be if she delayed her release until she couldn't hold back any longer.

At the same time he rubbed her hot-spot deep inside, Ty pressed his palm flat on her lower belly on the outside of her body, making every stroke against her G-spot that much more tactile. Then he moved his thumb over her clit and rolled the tiny bud in small circles.

"Ohmigod, Ty…I can't."

She began to buck hard against him.

"Look at me."

Evan opened her eyes and the arousal he saw there almost did him in. Ty clenched his jaw and reined in his raging lust. If he didn't, the woman wouldn't know what hit her. He'd be inside her before her orgasm stopped.

She'd risen up on her hands to press her body down hard against the heel of his hand. As her channel began to contract around his fingers, her arms began to shake and Ty couldn't resist any longer. While he continued to stroke inside her body, he cupped the back of her neck and yanked her close.

When his mouth covered hers, Evan wrapped her arms around his shoulders. As she rode the last remnants of her climax, she tugged on his hair, moaned against his mouth and pressed closer. If that didn't tell him just how much she enjoyed what he was doing to her, nothing would.

The momentum of her actions threw them both back against the bed. Ty was so caught up he reacted purely on animal instinct.

Withdrawing his hand from her body, he quickly rolled her underneath him. His fingers speared through her hair at the same time he thrust his tongue deep in her mouth. Without conscious thought he pressed his aching cock against her wet heat and ground against her. He relished the sensation of her naked breasts crushed against his chest, while the smell of her sex further seduced him with its alluring aroma.

Evan panted at his actions and dug her fingernails into his back. She wrapped her legs tight around his hips and locked him to her.

Ty pistoned against her sweet body as if his hips had a mind all their own. His jeans did little to buffer the erotic sensations his actions elicited. When he felt his orgasm approaching and realized his mind wasn't going to be able slow it down, he jerked his mouth from hers. No, it wasn't supposed to happen like this. He was determined to remain detached, in control.

He ignored the confused look on Evan's face as he got up from the bed.

"Ty?"

She sat up on her elbows. Her breasts were begging to be touched, her hair was a gorgeous mess and her lips were swollen from his hard kisses. He wanted nothing more than to sink into her body again and again. The thought of being the very first man to do so slammed through his mind, front and center. But not like this. Not when he didn't have a handle on his desires.

"My way," was all he managed to grunt out before he grabbed his boots and walked out of the bedroom, heading for the front door.

Chapter Six

Evan stood in her house and shoved clothes across the wooden rod in her bedroom closet with a disgruntled sigh. Nothing. Not one damn stylish piece of clothing in the whole lot.

"What does that say about you?" she mumbled aloud as she blew an errant curl out of her face.

She glanced at her watch and her stomach tensed when she realized she had less than two hours to transform herself into a sleek, sophisticated woman before Harm and Jena's party started. Harm's parents were very active in the community, so she knew everyone who was anyone would be there…including Doctor Lily Shelton. It irked her that she felt this strong desire to outshine Lily.

She pulled a blue dress she'd forgotten about out of the closet. Laying the soft fabric against her chest, she turned and faced herself in the mirror.

She scanned the freckles on her nose then moved her gaze to her broad shoulders and mammoth height, and came to the annoying conclusion she couldn't compete with Lily's sleek, classy look and petite stature.

Throwing the dress on her bed, she frowned at herself in the mirror. Why was it so important that she grab Ty's attention tonight? Her cheeks turned red at the memory of what they shared earlier. The passion and intensity between them blew her away. Ty did what he set out to do. He showed her that a man with the right sexual knowledge could make her body quake with a mind-blowing orgasm.

But what swept her heart away wasn't only the soul-jarring climax she'd experienced, but Ty's lips on hers, the sensation of him rolling her underneath him and pressing his cock against her as if he couldn't stop himself. In that moment, she realized that more than losing her virginity, what she wanted from Ty was fierce, unbridled, out-of-control desire—for her. Something she had a depressing feeling he once felt and, based on his reaction today, probably still felt for Lily.

With one last determined glance at the mirror, she squared her shoulders and turned back to the closet to find a pair of shoes.

* * * * *

Ty kept one eye on the hotel's ballroom doorway while he half listened to his mom talking to Harm's parents.

"Having a good time, Ty?" His uncle Rick clapped him on the shoulder as he walked up.

Ty turned to his uncle. "Hey, Uncle Rick. I'm glad you made it. Have you spoken to Jena yet?"

Rick gave him a broad smile. The effect spread his black mustache across his open face. "Yep, met her fiancé, too. She seems very happy." His smile lowered and a sad look crossed his face. "I wish my brother had lived to see his little girl getting married."

Ty put his hand on his uncle's thick shoulder. "I think my dad would be very glad to know his brother came all the way to Texas to see his niece get married."

His uncle's smile returned. "I know you're giving Jena away, but I told her I'd like to stand up and give her a kiss and a hug for her dad before she takes her vows."

Ty nodded and smiled. "I'm sure she'd love that."

Turning to Harm's parents who Jena had introduced him to earlier, Ty said, "Mr. and Mrs. Steele, I'd like you to meet our uncle, Rick Hudson."

While Rick spoke to Harm's parents, Ty pushed his suit jacket sleeve back and glanced at his watch. Where was Evan? The party had started half an hour ago. Guilt tightened his chest.

He'd left her rather abruptly. When he'd come back to the house, she was gone. He hoped the reason she hadn't shown yet wasn't because she was upset at the way he'd left. But damn the woman affected him more than he wanted or expected her to.

Familiar seductive floral perfume with a hint of jasmine surrounded him before a feminine hand encircled the crook of his arm.

"Hello, Ty."

His gaze locked with Lily's dark brown eyes and his stomach tensed. "Hey, Lily."

She kept her hand on his arm and her gaze drifted across his face. "You left before I could tell you to keep your wound clean, and if you're still in town after two weeks, to come back to have the stitches removed."

Ty didn't respond. He scanned the crowd sitting down and eating, then his gaze moved past the group of people dancing on the dance floor to the entrance once more.

"You're so quiet. Not at all like the Ty I knew."

Ty heard the knowing smile in her tone. He didn't bother looking down at her when he responded. "I'm not the same person I was back then."

"I'm sure you aren't. You're a grown man now." She tugged on his arm. "You seem so tense. Come dance with me for old times' sake."

Ty allowed her to pull him out on the dance floor. He felt like a piece of hard metal bent to its limit, ready to snap, but the sensation of her hand on his arm told him he needed to find out for sure if he'd finally gotten over her. How would it feel to hold her in his arms again after all these years?

As he put his arm around Lily's lower back and held her other hand to lead, he noted just how small and fragile she was. Even wearing three-inch heels she just reached his chin. Tonight she'd worn her straight black hair down. The soft strands landed just over her shoulders. Her black spaghetti-strapped dress scooped low to reveal her ample cleavage—cleavage he'd very much appreciated as a randy teenager.

"This suit looks custom-made." Lily's gaze followed her hand as she ran it across his shoulder to feel the expensive black fabric. A pleased smile crossed her features as she met his gaze. "So you're an architect who owns his own business. You've done very well for yourself."

He raised his eyebrow at her comment. "You've been checking up on me?"

She laughed. "How else was I supposed to find out? It's not like you were forthcoming with your background information."

Ty shrugged. "It wasn't relevant."

"True. But I was curious. Weren't you ever curious about me? Curious to know how I turned out?"

His entire body tensed. How many times had he wondered what had happened to Lily? What type of man it took to make her happy? "Not really."

A hurt expression crossed her face. "You asked me to marry you once, Ty. Are you saying I meant so little to you?"

Ty's jaw tightened. "That was a long time ago."

Her lips thinned as if she were irritated by his abrupt tone before a smile settled on her lips. "Yes, it was a long time ago. We were both very young, but one thing has stayed with me all these years."

"What was that?"

Lily slid her arm up his shoulder and cupped the back of his neck. Pressing her chest against his, she pulled on his neck until he moved close enough for her to whisper in his ear.

"You're the best lover I ever had."

Shock ricocheted through Ty at her revelation. All the time he'd spent thinking he didn't measure up. All those years of sexual self-doubt in his early twenties, wondering if his performance in the sack was the reason he couldn't convince Lily to marry him.

At the same time he straightened to look Lily in the face, he caught sight of Evan standing ten feet away, staring at him.

Evan started to walk away, but Chad grasped her elbow. The jerk-off whispered something in her ear before he clasped her hand and tugged her out onto the dance floor.

Lily's soft fingers turned Ty's jaw until his gaze met hers. "Did you hear what I said?" Her dark gaze searched his as she wrapped her arms around his neck.

Ty stopped dancing and pulled her arms down from his neck. "Like you said…we were just kids."

Lily gave him a siren's smile. Her seductive gaze swept over him, assessing and appreciating every inch. "Oh, I know that. If you were good back then with no sexual experience, I can only imagine what you're like now."

Her words landed on him like a load of wet cement, heavy and sticky but quickly turning hard and stiff. And here he thought she'd dumped him because he was a lousy lay. He closed his eyes for a brief second.

As anger swept through him, Ty opened his eyes and his gaze drifted back to Chad's arms around Evan's waist. The jackass had started massaging her back. Her wavy hair just brushed her exposed back where her navy dress plunged all the way to the base of her spine.

When Ty looked at Evan, his pulse raced and he instantly went hard…no matter what she wore. Then again, he liked her best wearing nothing at all. The better to enjoy her long legs and miles of sweet, honey-toned skin.

"Ty."

He forced his gaze away from Evan and Chad at the pout in Lily's tone. As he narrowed his gaze on the woman before him, Ty realized two certainties—just how much he wanted Evan and just how fucking over Lily he was. She didn't hold a candle to the way Evan made him feel…made him burn with the need to touch her.

"You got what you wanted in life…no one to hold you back from your professional goals, Doctor Shelton. I hope you're happy with it."

Ty walked off the dance floor and headed straight for the bar. "Shot of whisky, straight up."

The bartender nodded and poured him a drink.

Ty watched Chad lean close and brush his lips down Evan's neck. He picked up the shot glass and downed the drink in one swig. Fury, unlike anything he'd ever experienced in his life swept through him, burning just like the alcohol did going down. Everything he'd learned, breathing techniques, focus, emotional control—gone. All because a man dared to touch the woman he wanted.

Wanted.

Hell yeah, he wanted Evan. Wanted to feel her long, shapely legs wrapped around his hips, wanted to hear her moaning as he slid inside her, then screaming when he began to thrust deep. He wanted her to come over and over…all because of him.

Gritting his teeth, he was glad his jacket covered the raging hard-on that pushed against the fly of his pants.

Lily chose that moment to walk up and order a glass of white wine. Her gaze followed his line of sight. After the bartender poured her glass, she picked it up and took a sip.

She turned to walk away, but paused just a moment to glance at him over her shoulder. "Since I doubt you'll be coming by my office to have your stitches removed, why don't you ask Doctor Masters to take care of removing them for you."

Ty frowned at the sarcasm in Lily's voice. Was she jealous that he was interested in someone who didn't hold a professional job? Evan seemed very dedicated to her career, regardless if she didn't have initials by her last name. Even though he used that as an excuse to give Lily a hard time, Ty didn't give a shit about the professional part. It all boiled down to the fact he was a selfish bastard. He didn't want a woman who sent him to the backseat for her career.

Jena's voice drew his attention. "You've put in an appearance, big brother. You can leave any time you'd like."

Ty slid his gaze her way. "What makes you think I want to leave?"

She gave him a sisterly smile. "Oh, I dunno. Maybe because you haven't taken your eyes off Evan since she walked in the room."

Ty looked down at the shot glass he rolled in his palm. "You afraid I'm going to make another scene?"

"Are you?"

When he snapped his gaze to hers, mischief danced in his sister's vivid blue eyes.

The slow song was coming to the end. A devilish smile tugged at Ty's lips as he set the shot glass on the counter. "Not as long as I can pry Evan out of the cocky bastard's tight clutches."

"Allow me." Before Ty could say a word, his sister started across the dance floor toward the couple.

"Chad, I'm so glad to see you could make it." Jena walked up with her hand outstretched and a broad smile on her face.

Chad shifted his gaze to their hostess and put his hand out to shake Jena's hand. "Hey, Jena, or should I say, Soon-to-be Mrs. Harmon Steele. Thanks for the invitation."

Jena tugged on Chad's hand. "Your dad wanted me to introduce you to my family. My Uncle Rick's an attorney. I told him you'd just passed the bar. Come and meet him."

Chad's grip on Evan's waist started to slip as he allowed Jena to tug him toward her. Evan knew Chad planned to follow in his father's political footsteps. He was also the kind of guy who never passed up an opportunity to make another contact. In that respect, he was definitely his father's son.

"You finally made it." The sound of Ty's deep voice made Evan's heart skip several beats.

Chad's grip on her waist instantly tightened when he heard Ty behind them. He turned and narrowed his gaze on Jena's brother. "Evan's here with me."

Evan stepped out of Chad's hold, angry with both men. "I'm not 'here' with anyone." Nodding toward Jena, she smiled. "I take it the rehearsal went well?"

Jena laughed as she tucked her hand around Chad's arm. "Of course, but despite a great rehearsal, I know one should never expect everything to go perfectly on one's wedding day."

Evan smiled her understanding then looked up at Chad. "Go with Jena."

His blue gaze darted between Evan and Ty before it narrowed. "I'll go if you promise me a dance tomorrow after the wedding."

She felt the weight of Ty's heavy gaze on her, but she refused to look his way. "Okay, I'll dance with yo—"

Chad pulled her close and kissed her hard, cutting off her words. Evan didn't even have time to react. Chad broke their kiss and cast a triumphant smirk Ty's way before he walked off with Jena.

Evan's stomach tightened at Ty's nearness, but anger still welled within her. She'd seen the way Lily had herself wrapped around him. Ty didn't seem to mind one bit. As a matter of fact, he seemed to have a tight grip on the woman's perfectly pinched, no-wider-than-the-span-of-a-man's-hand waist. Grrrr!

"Evan."

She ignored him as she headed for the entryway. She'd come to the party as she promised Jena she would, but she refused to hang with Ty. It wasn't like they had any type of commitment or anything, but for God's sake the man had had his hand inside her, stroking her to climax just a few hours ago. Her heels clicked on the hard floor outside the ballroom with each determined step she took down the hall toward the hotel's entrance.

"Evan."

Her stomach fluttered at the sound of Ty's voice so close behind her. "It's okay, Ty. I've decided to let you off the hook from our agreement."

Evan gasped when Ty grabbed her arm and opened a door that led to an empty ballroom. Yanking her inside, he closed the door and faced her. The dim lighting in the room allowed her to see the anger reflected in his expression as he jerked his head back toward the way they had come.

"Why? Because you'd rather have that prick's cock in you instead?"

The sound of Evan's hand connecting with Ty's face resounded in the large empty room. "That was outta line."

Ty grabbed her wrist before she could pull away. His green gaze glittered with anger and something else as he used his hold to yank her toward him.

When his mouth landed on hers, hard and demanding, Evan let out a surprised yelp, which came out sounding like a muffled "hmmmph". Ty's lips didn't just claim hers. He possessed her with his aggressive kiss. His tongue thrust deep in her mouth and his hands moved to her back before they slid down her spine to cup her rear through her dress. It was the kind of kiss that had nothing to do with control and everything to do with unleashed, raw, staking-his-claim desire.

But as excited as Ty's kiss made her, she wasn't about to let the man insult her without giving as good as she got. Pushing against his chest, she broke their heated kiss. "Don't you think Lily will wonder where you went?"

He gave her a puzzled look. "What are you talking about?"

She tried to pull out of his arms, but Ty just tightened his hold.

"Answer me, damn it."

Evan shrugged at the anger in his tone. "Jena told me you and Lily dated a long time ago. I guess when you saw her all dressed up, you decided to pick up where you left off."

Ty's gaze dropped to her lips and he backed her up against the door. "There's only one woman I want."

With her back flat against the door, Ty pressed his chest against her breasts and finished in a husky tone, "You're the only woman I'm so hot to get inside of I can't think about anything else." He pressed his lips to her neck and lifted her off the floor so he could rock his erection against her mound. "I can't wait to slide inside your sweet, tight body, Eve."

His words went straight to her toes and her pulse thrummed in excitement. Evan cupped the back of his neck as his lips covered hers once more. When he set her down and his hands began to lift the hem of her dress higher, her heart hammered and her lower belly tensed in pent-up sexual frustration. Of their own accord, her hands moved to unbutton his jacket then she slid her hands down his tight stomach to unbutton and unzip his pants. She didn't give a damn if her first time was against a door…so long as it was with Ty and just like this—as passionate at it could be.

His warm hands connected with the back of her bare legs, sending shivers down her spine. Evan moaned against his mouth. Her sounds must've spurred him on because he gripped her thighs and lifted her. Before she could utter a word, he rammed his cloth-covered cock against her. Her underwear and his boxer briefs prevented what they both seemed to desperately want, yet the barrier of clothes between them somehow turned her on even more.

As he began to rock against her, she wrapped her arms and legs tight around him, pausing to say between heated kisses, "I think we're a bit overdressed."

"Shhhh," he said then moved his lips near her ear. His thrusts grew stronger as he rode her against the door. "You're so damn wet. God, I'm so fucking aroused by your heat." His grip tightened on her buttocks and his shoulders tensed underneath her arms as he ground himself against her. She cried out at the erotic sensations building inside her.

Ty's breath expelled in a hiss as if he were trying his best not to lose it. He lowered her to the ground and she felt his knuckles rubbing her sex as he shoved his cock through the opening in his boxers.

Evan's heart pounded even faster when Ty slid his fingers down her mound to cup her in a possessive hold. The sensation of his fingers skimming across her sex outside her wet underwear only made her heart beat harder. She gripped his shoulders and felt them suddenly tense underneath her fingers.

"Wait. I've got a condom."

She shook her head. "No, don't stop. I'm on the Pill."

A surprised expression crossed his face. "A virgin on the Pill?"

She panted, "It keeps me regular."

Ty nodded and ground out, "I'm glad I don't have to stop." His intense gaze locked with hers at the same time he jerked her underwear to the side. Her heart pounded in excited, stuttering jolts at his aggressive action and the sensation of his hand moving between them to grasp his erection.

"Has anyone seen Evan?" a man called down the hall, his voice frantic as he ran past.

Evan froze, her heart pounding out of control. She pushed on Ty's chest. "I'm sorry. I have to go."

Ty held her tight for a couple of seconds as if he didn't want to let her go. When he finally he released her, Evan straightened her underwear and lowered her dress before she opened the door and closed it behind her.

"Dave, over here."

Ty quickly fixed his pants and buttoned his jacket then exited the room. When he closed the door behind him he saw an older man in a bloodstained T-shirt standing a few feet away talking to Evan in rapid bursts.

"She's bleeding everywhere.

"That nasty dog attacked her.

"Please, Evan, you've got to save our little Sadie."

"Calm down, Dave." Evan put a hand on the man's arm.

The gray-haired man took a couple of deep breaths and nodded. "I'm calm."

She pulled her hand away and gave him a reassuring smile. "Good. Where is Sadie now?"

The old man's hand shook as he pointed toward the entrance to the hotel lobby. "She's wrapped in a towel in the car. My wife's holding her."

Evan patted his shoulder. "Okay. Bring her straight to my office. I'll meet you there in just a few minutes."

Her office? "Is the vet back in town then?" Ty asked.

The old man gave him a confused look. "Huh?" He pointed to Evan. "She *is* the vet," he said before he took off running back toward the lobby.

Ty met Evan's gaze and saw the truth in her eyes. "You're the town vet?" The comment Lily made to him earlier now made perfect sense. She must've assumed he knew Evan was a vet and wanted to dig at him for choosing Evan over her.

Evan gave him a half-smile. "Guilty." A moment of silence stretched between them. Hearing Evan confirm Dave's words, Ty was so surprised, he didn't know what to say.

Evan pushed a lock of hair behind her ear. "I'd better go meet Dave. It sounds like Sadie's pretty torn up."

As shocked as he was by this latest discovery about Evan's career, Ty wasn't ready to let her go. "Is there anything I can do to help? Bring you some clothes?"

"I always keep a change of clothes in my car." She smiled and started to turn away, calling over her shoulder, "I'll see you later, okay?"

"Sure."

While Evan rushed toward the entrance of the hotel, Ty's gaze locked on her sweet ass swaying to the click of her heels. His groin tightened all over again when she cast her gaze back at him one last time before she walked outside. Once Evan was out of sight, the realization he'd almost lost complete control with her against the door in the ballroom sank in full force. Damn, she'd had him so caught up. Ty locked his jaw, both annoyed and relieved at the interruption.

Why had she lied to him about her profession? He steeled himself, his shoulders tensing in sheer determination. He would find out the answer…and he would damn well hold his emotions in check when they had sex. This time around he was going into it with his eyes wide open. No expectations, no strings attached, period. Evan would get what she wanted and so would he — a roll in the hay with a gorgeous woman who was turning out to be made up of layers he never would've imagined.

* * * * *

Evan walked inside the Double D's ranch house as quietly as she could. It was almost eleven. The emergency surgery had taken a lot longer than she'd anticipated, but she'd managed to save the mangled dog. Sadie would look like a refugee for a while, but Evan hoped the small pooch thought twice before tangling with a dog seven times her size again.

Ty was asleep on the couch. Even though he had the air-conditioning cranked up, he slept with no shirt and a thin sheet covering his lower body. She walked up to stare at his gorgeous chest for a few seconds.

The memory of their encounter in the empty ballroom would be burned in her head for a long time to come — the intensity and sheer spontaneity had blown her away. And still…he seemed to hold back a little. A smile tilted the corners of her lips. At least she got to see and feel some of his steely control slip down a notch or two.

Evan let out a quiet sigh and headed for her bedroom and a much-needed shower.

After she'd pulled off her clothes, she stepped under the pounding spray. The hot water pelted her skin like warm, soothing fingers massaging her tired muscles.

She wished she could read Ty's mind when he found out she was the town vet. He definitely looked surprised, but he hadn't appeared put off by it. If anything, he'd appeared intrigued. At least Ty seemed to accept her vet status.

She started to pick up her soap but her gaze strayed to Ty's bar of soap sitting next to hers in the dish attached to the wall.

Evan couldn't resist picking up the brown-hued bar and inhaling. It smelled of sandalwood and other spices she couldn't identify. She ran his soap over her skin and reveled in Ty's scent floating in the air around her. She lifted her forearm, put her nose to her freshly washed skin and inhaled deeply. Her stomach tensed and her heart jerked at the appealing scent. She'd have to ask him what brand the soap was so she could buy some. Then she could keep a bit of Ty with her long after he left.

The thought of Ty leaving made her chest constrict as she shampooed her hair and rinsed the suds out. *Get a grip, girl. You haven't even had sex with the man yet.* But it wasn't just about the sex with Ty. He was intelligent and seductively intense. He stuck to his convictions and stepped in without a moment's hesitation for those who needed help. He was exactly the type of man she wanted to marry one day.

Too bad he lived fifteen hundred miles away. She shut the shower off with a determined twist of her wrist. At least she had him for a couple more days. The sight of the water draining out of the shower, steam floating in the air and Ty's scent lingering in the room conjured the memory of Ty stroking his erection during his shower.

He'd seemed so in command of himself and his physical responses. The sheer restraint was a turn-on unlike any she'd ever seen. Her vivid thoughts made her sex throb in excited awareness. Shrugging off the seductive sensations gripping her on both a mental and physical level, Evan grabbed the towel off the shower rod and wrapped it around herself.

Once she'd towel-dried her hair, she tucked the towel's end between her breasts and pulled the shower curtain back. Evan let out a small gasp, her heart racing at the sight of Ty standing in the doorway in his black boxer briefs. He leaned against the doorjamb, not at all embarrassed by his obvious erection pushing the cotton material outward.

He didn't say a word as he walked toward her. Evan's pulse leapt at the rugged look of his tousled dark hair and five o'clock shadow. He entered her personal space and his green gaze studied her with a palpable heat that made her breath catch in her throat. When he reached for the towel's end tucked between her breasts, her stomach flip-flopped then did a triple somersault. As he grasped the fabric, his knuckles nudged her cleavage. The erotic sensation made her knees threaten to give way.

Ty's gaze dropped to her body while he peeled the towel away. He scanned every inch in a slow, leisurely sweep.

Chill bumps formed on her skin while she waited to see his eyes again. What would she see reflected in their deep green depths?

But Ty didn't return his gaze to hers. Instead, he surprised her when he dropped the towel on the floor and swiftly picked her up, carrying her out of the bathroom.

Evan's pulse raced as her arms settled around his broad shoulders. Defined muscles flexed underneath her hands. She ran her palms across his warm skin and inhaled. Ty's scent reached out and grabbed her at a deep, gut-wrenching level. She pressed her nose against his neck and took another deep breath. Evan realized that no soap could ever capture Ty's true essence. His own masculine smell mingled with the soap's aroma to create a scent that totally seduced her.

Ty laid her down on the bed and then straightened to step out of his boxers. When his underwear hit the floor, her gaze locked on his hard erection and her lower belly clenched in response. The man was definitely well-endowed. Her breath hitched when the bed dipped as he placed his knee on the bed.

His hands hit the mattress on either side of her head as he leaned over her. While the light from the bathroom cast his face in dark shadows, she knew her face was fully exposed. She didn't care. Let him see the desire in her gaze. Maybe it would help him open up a little. Evan placed her hands on his shoulders as he moved closer. She held her breath, waiting.

Ty's lips brushed against hers in a feather-light kiss. Her fingers flexed on his shoulders as she pressed her mouth against his, ready for more. She ran her tongue along his lower lip and a low growl rumbled against her mouth before Ty pulled away and lay down behind her.

He cupped her breast and used his hold to pull her back flush against his hard chest, aligning his muscular body with hers. Evan sighed in excited anticipation.

She felt him rub his nose in her hair and heard him inhale her scent. Her heart skipped several beats as she waited.

And waited.

A few seconds later, her anticipation turned to disappointment. She felt Ty's erection against her backside. His fingers were sure to leave imprints on her breast, he held her in such a firm grip, yet the man remained perfectly still.

She reached back and slid her fingers up his neck, then speared them through his thick, silky hair.

"Ty?"

"Shhh," he whispered against her neck. His heated breath sent shivers skidding down her spine. He released her breast to pull the covers over them then clasped her hip under the covers in a possessive hold.

Still he didn't move.

Her body ached so much for him, her lower belly began to cramp. Evan closed her eyes for a brief second, seeking patience.

She failed miserably.

"Are we sleeping?" She tried to keep the frustration out of her voice.

Ty pressed his erection against her buttocks as he flattened his palm across her belly. "Yeah, we are. You've had a long day and night. You need to rest."

I need you sliding inside me, she wanted to scream.

She turned over onto her back. "Is this another 'my way' thing?"

He chuckled and kissed her on the forehead. "I guess it is."

Evan faced him and hooked her leg across his thigh.

Shoving Ty on his back, she straddled his hips then rested her sex against his erection. "Hell no. Tonight we're doing things *my* way."

Chapter Seven

She felt the tension in Ty's chest underneath her palms as his hands surrounded her hips.

"I know you're exhausted, Evan. We can wait until tomorrow."

Determination washed over her and she began to rock her hips, rubbing her hot moisture along the length of his cock.

The veins in Ty's neck surfaced and his fingers tightened on her hips, slowing her movements. "Evan," he warned. The light behind her, now that their positions were switched, revealed the heated desire burning in his gaze and the look of tension on his face. The man wanted her and was mentally working through fighting his desire. The realization made her want him that much more.

Evan leaned forward and touched her nipples to his chest as she whispered against his ear, "Tonight, no more holding back." At the same time she lowered her entrance against the tip of his cock.

When her soft heat came in contact with his body, Ty's hips jerked. His action caused his erection to barely slide inside her. It was a surprising, seductive tease.

Evan bit back her moan. She planted a kiss on his neck and lowered her body fully against his, blanketing him with her skin. "I want to feel your body against mine when you slide inside me. I've waited long enough."

Demanding hands gripped her hips and his lips grazed her neck. "Then it'll be my way," he ground out as his hips began to rock.

Evan felt his thickness moving deeper inside her, his actions slow, measured, precise. She moaned at the wonderful sensation, but she also realized he was doing it again—taking control while keeping himself in a kind of buffered state, as if he wanted their physical joining without losing control of himself in the process.

"I told you we're doing it my way." Before Ty could stop her, she put her hands on his shoulders and shoved his hard shaft deep inside her channel, joining their bodies.

Her swift movement made Ty fill and stretch her completely. Piercing pain shot though her walls, making her eyes water. She gulped back her scream and buried her head against his shoulder.

"Damn it, Evan!" Ty's hands slid from her hips to cup her buttocks.

She heard the anger and censure in his tone, but Evan didn't care. She wanted him to let go, to totally give in to his desires—all of them.

Neither one of them moved for a few seconds.

Ty kissed her temple. "Are you okay?"

The pain had subsided to a dull ache. Evan nodded her head then pushed herself to a seated position.

Her aggressive change of position caused his cock to hit her womb. She winced at the sharp pain.

Ty slid his hands to her upper back. "Give yourself more of an angle, sweetheart," he said in a husky tone at the same time he pulled her forward.

Evan bent her elbows a little and did as he suggested. Sheer pleasure quickly replaced the ache. She closed her eyes and moaned, savoring the decadent sensation of Ty's hard erection buried so deep, filling her wall to wall.

Though he'd moved his hands back to her hips, Ty hadn't said a word. Evan opened her eyes as she began to rock her hips.

Ty's eyes were closed and the tendons on his neck stood out as his hold on her hips tightened. She could tell he was concentrating.

"Look at me," she whispered. She had to see the desire in his eyes, to know he felt something more than what his body was telling her.

Ty's green gaze locked with hers and the tortured look almost took her breath away. It was as if he wanted so badly to let go, but he couldn't allow himself the luxury.

"You may be leaving day after tomorrow, but I'm determined you'll be flying out of Texas well spent, Ty Hudson. You feel too damn good and I plan to keep you in bed as long as I can."

The color of his eyes shifted to a green so dark his eyes looked black. He flashed her a sexy grin as he began to thrust upward with each of her downward movements.

Evan arched her back at his aggressive and very effective movements. She felt stretched and full and very fulfilled. Her breasts tingled and her heart raced while her entire body flushed with renewed heat.

When Ty feathered his fingers across her nipples, her entire belly clenched in excited anticipation. "Touch me," she whispered.

Ty's gaze held hers as he rolled her nipples between his fingers. Evan's rocking pace increased and her breathing came out in short, erratic pants. Exquisite pleasure shot through her body.

She closed her eyes.

"Open your eyes. I want to watch you come."

Her eyes flew open at his comment.

"You were right. You're helluva lot tighter than your mouth," he said in a strained tone.

"And you're a helluva lot bigger than my fingers," she panted back with a half-laugh.

When she finished speaking, Ty thrust hard and deep at the same time he pinched her nipples. "The better to make you scream."

The deep timbre of his voice skidded down her spine while all the sensations slamming into her at once caused tremors of pleasure to scatter throughout her body. Delicious sexual arousal built to its highest pitch within her.

Wave after wave of sheer ecstasy started in her channel and splintered all the way down to her fingers and her toes in heated, tingling bursts as her orgasm took over.

Ty moved his hands to her hips and used his grip to bury himself even deeper while she gyrated her hips, wanting her orgasm to last forever. "That's it, sweetheart. Take all of me."

And Evan did. She pushed down, pressing her body hard against Ty's, taking him into her as deep as she could. She rode her explosive climax until the wonderful tremors stopped and her body shook all over in the aftermath.

Sweat glistened on Ty's chest. He was still hard and impaled so far inside her that she felt his heartbeat at the base of his cock. The rapid thump told her what he refused to…just how much he wanted to let go.

She leaned forward and planted a kiss on his hard chest, then flicked her tongue around his nipple until the tiny nub raised up enough for her to nip at it with her teeth.

Ty moaned and his hips jerked at her stimulation. One hand threaded through her hair, cupping the back of her head while the other caressed her rear.

Evan turned her head and laid it next to Ty's for a brief second to catch her breath. Ty's heart pounded against her chest. She smiled at the telltale sign then pushed herself back to a seated position.

Her gaze locked with his. "Ready to go for a ride, Yank?"

Ty cocked his eyebrow at her comment. Before he could respond she pulled herself completely off him, then slammed back down, burying him to the hilt.

"Shit, Evan!" he ground out as his hips moved of their own accord. He gave as good as he got, but Evan refused to climax without him this time.

"This ride doesn't stop until you're over the edge."

Ty groaned. "Is that a challenge?"

"No, it's a promise." Evan gave him a siren's smile as she reached behind her and cupped his sac in a firm grip.

Ty grunted and a surprised expression filtered across his face. "Easy," he warned with a half-groan, half-chuckle.

"I know a bit or two about male physiology." Her smile widened and she ran two fingers past his sac to press on the sensitive skin underneath them.

Ty let out a low growl. Before she knew what hit her, Ty sat up and had her back flat against the bed. He'd moved so fast he took her breath away.

His hands speared through her hair and his mouth slanted across her lips at the same time his body covered hers.

Evan moaned and accepted his first deep thrust with relish. She put her feet flat on the bed and raised her hips, ready for him to withdraw and piston into her again and again. This was exactly what she wanted…Ty letting go.

Ty pulled out and rammed into her once more. His stubble scraped the soft skin around her mouth as his tongue tangled with hers. His kiss was hungry, dark, possessive and so utterly seductive that for a few seconds she just lay there kissing him while their bodies remained locked together, throbbing, waiting for them to move.

"Think you can handle me?" His rampant breathing was hot against her neck.

Evan ran her hands across his muscular back and down his spine until she cupped his muscular buttocks. "If you're not thrusting hard enough, I'm gonna tell ya, darlin'."

Ty let out a strained chuckle then planted a kiss on her neck. "Don't worry. I want you so fucking bad I just thought you should have fair warning."

When he finished, he began to move his hips, each thrust harder and deeper than the last. His pace was rough and hard and, damn, it felt so good.

Evan relished the sensation of his muscular chest pressing her to the bed as his body moved inside her. The entire experience felt erotic, heated and so very right with Ty. His body ground against her clitoris, driving her insane with intense pleasure. She began to pant as her heart hammered out of control.

"Bend your knees and wrap them around me."

Evan wasn't sure where he was going with his command, but she wrapped her legs around his hips.

Ty's breathing came out in harsh gusts. "Hold your legs as high as you can."

She didn't really want to change her position. It felt pretty damn good just the way she was.

Ty kissed her jaw then the soft spot behind her ear. "The angle will send you through the roof."

"When you put it that way..." She grabbed her shins and pulled them higher up his back. At the same time Ty came down with a forceful thrust.

Evan let out a keening moan as her body instantly began to spasm around him once more. This time her orgasm seemed to go bone-deep. Evan's heart thrummed at a jackrabbit's pace as her body contracted around Ty's erection again and again.

Ty grunted and fisted his hand in her hair while he buried his nose in the damp strands on the other side of her head. A low groan escaped his lips as he came, his hips pinning her to the bed with each ramming thrust.

With her own orgasm subsiding, Evan let go of her shins and locked her ankles at the base of Ty's back. She held him as close as she could until his movements stopped.

Evan was amazed at the intensity of their lovemaking. Sweat coated their skin. Ty's heart thundered against her chest as she lowered her legs and tangled them with his.

She didn't know what to expect once the tide of sheer passion settled between them. But it felt so good just to lie there entangled in each other. Ty laid his forehead on her shoulder as he pressed himself even deeper inside her.

"That was amaz—"

Ty's lips covered hers, cutting off her words. He kissed her until she lost track of her train of thought. When she sighed against his mouth, he withdrew from her body and rolled over onto his side. Wrapping his arm around her waist, he gathered her close and pressed her back against his chest.

Evan didn't mind. As sweaty as they were, she snuggled against his hips. Aligning her legs with his, she laid her hand over his much larger one that now rested on her hip.

He kissed her cheek then spoke next to her ear. "Tomorrow morning I want to know why you lied to me about you being a vet."

She laced her fingers with his. "Only if you tell me what you have against sleeping with virgins."

She felt Ty stiffen behind her for a brief second. "It's not the same thing."

Evan shrugged. She refused to let him evade her question. "Consider it tit for tat."

"You push too far."

She tensed at his detached tone. He was withdrawing again. She wouldn't let him put up his barrier once more.

"You'll be leaving day after tomorrow. Let's just drop it."

His hand flexed on her hip then his grip tightened for a brief second. "The wedding starts at ten tomorrow. We'd better get some sleep."

Evan closed her eyes and inhaled. For now she'd just relish being surrounded by Ty's scent and muscular body. They were perfect physically and she found him intellectually interesting. But neither one of them seemed to be willing to share something deeper about themselves. It was such a shame. Ty made her heart sing on so many levels.

Ty listened to Evan's tiny snores as she slept. He smiled in the dark and ran his hand down her thigh and back up. She muttered something and then started to roll over onto her belly.

For some reason he couldn't fathom, a feeling of emptiness came over him at the thought of Evan pulling away from him.

He captured her shoulder and rolled her over. Pushing her head on his chest, he lay on his back and gathered her close.

While she slept, Evan naturally settled her head on his shoulder and flung her arm across his waist and her thigh over his.

He closed his eyes and fought the possessive thoughts that rushed forth. She was his. No man, not Chad, not anyone, would have her.

As much as he wanted to stand on the rooftop and beat his chest marking his territory, he had to face reality. Evan was a very independent woman. She owned her own successful business and many people depended on her, even if they didn't give her the respectful title of "doctor" that she very much deserved.

She didn't seem to have a need for a man in her life other than to help her with the whole virginity thing. Why had she lied to him about being a vet? Did she think the discovery would make him want to stick around? That it made her a greater catch? He stiffened at the insulting thought. But it kind of made sense in a weird sort of way. As a visitor, he was the perfect person to have no-strings-attached sex with. She could get the deed out of the way without any worry of commitment.

That's what he wanted too, wasn't it? Mind-blowing, no-strings-attached sex. Correction…very long, drawn-out, blue-ball eliciting, sexually frustrating moments that culminated into fan-fucking-tastic sex. He couldn't believe the woman really yanked on his balls! And that she knew running her fingers down his sac and below would send him over the edge. Damn, sex with Evan felt so good…like her tight little channel and adventurous nature were the perfect match for him.

He clenched his teeth and forced the possessive thoughts from his head. He'd learned his lesson about getting emotionally involved in the past. He refused to make the same mistake twice. Come Sunday he'd be on a plane back to Maryland.

Then why couldn't he get enough of Evan's natural cinnamon and vanilla scent? he wondered as he buried his nose in Evan's tangled, damp, curly hair and inhaled. His stomach clenched as he realized his own smell now commingled with hers, and damn, it smelled good.

* * * * *

Evan awoke feeling sexually frustrated. All night she'd dreamed of Ty—the way his hands felt on her body, the sensation of his heated skin sliding along hers, his chest pressing against her breasts and his erection filling her to the hilt. He'd stretched her in so many delicious ways she was surprised she didn't wake swollen and sore. Instead, she awoke throbbing and aching for release.

She lifted her head and was disappointed to see the bed was empty beside her. When she glanced toward the window and saw the sun had barely begun to rise, she realized Ty must be outside doing his martial arts thing. At least that gave her a few minutes to herself. It would be better if she took the edge off than for Ty to think she was desperate for his touch again so soon.

Evan rolled onto her back and placed her feet flat on the bed. Closing her eyes, she skimmed her fingers past her breasts down her belly until they tangled in her soft hair between her thighs.

Thoughts of Ty entered her consciousness as the pads of her fingers found her clitoris.

Her heart rate inched upward when she began to massage the tiny sensitive nub.

She let out a small moan once she finally plunged a finger inside her channel. A frustrated sob escaped when she realized nothing would ever feel as good as Ty sliding inside her, his hard heat surrounding her while his rigid, thick cock plunged deep.

She kept up her pace and her sex reacted to the pleasant, if not majorly exciting, stimulation. She began to move her hips, hoping to rid herself of her body's addiction to Ty.

Evan's skin suddenly heated then chill bumps formed. The strangest sensation she was being watched washed over her. She opened her eyes to see Ty leaning against the doorjamb, watching her.

His chest was bare and his jeans were unbuttoned at the waist. She noted the distinct outline of his erection against the soft, worn denim.

Ty stared at her bent knee and the thigh that blocked his view. His green gaze locked with hers. He didn't smile, he just inclined his head. She realized what he was saying, "Lower your leg. I want to watch."

She slowly lowered her leg, but instead of staying in the position she was, she rolled over onto her belly, tossed her hair over her shoulder and arched her back. She glanced back at Ty for a brief second before she faced the headboard. She continued to touch herself but this time she rocked her hips even more. If asked, she wouldn't have been able to put it to words, but there was something incredibly sexy about Ty watching her. She wanted to make sure it was show he'd never forget.

When the mattress dipped, Evan paused her movements. Her heart hammered at the realization Ty was behind her on the bed. He was so close she felt his heat on her bare buttocks, but she didn't look back.

Ty's fingers feathered across the curve of her spine before his hands slid down her skin to cup her rear. Her pulse raced and her sex throbbed at the sound of his shallow breathing behind her. Ty placed his hands on her hips then he lifted them higher. She knew he was telling her to rise up on her knees. Evan complied, her body throbbing in anticipation. She let out a ragged breath and waited.

Ty's body heat spread across her spine as he rubbed his thumbs on the side of her buttocks. She realized he was leaning over her. When she felt his erection touch her entrance then begin to slide inside her, Evan closed her eyes in sexual bliss.

"You're pure temptation."

She shivered at his husky words. As her moist channel stretched to accept him, Evan panted out in amusement, "Is that why you called me Eve yesterday?" Coming from Ty, the nickname made her sound sensual and alluring, like a seductress.

"You're too smart for your own good." Ty thrust deep inside her then groaned, pushing his hips flush with hers.

Evan sobbed at the wonderful sensations ricocheting throughout her body. Somehow she managed to respond. "I've been told that a time or two." What an understatement!

Once he was seated fully inside her, Ty put his hands on her waist and slid his fingers up her rib cage until he cupped her breasts. Clasping her breasts in a firm grip, he pulled her to a kneeling position, aligning her body flush with his warm hard chest and muscular thighs.

"All I've thought about was sinking inside you again. Working out with a hard-on is *not* comfortable."

Evan chuckled at the frustration in his tone. Still she took a moment to inhale his masculine scent. He smelled of outdoors and musk—sexy and so very virile.

She was glad to know this out-of-control desire thing hadn't died with the new day upon them. If anything it seemed the rising sun only intensified how she felt about Ty, which scared her a little. She knew he didn't like Texas. Boone was her home and always would be.

Refusing to think beyond the moment, she tilted her head as he planted a kiss on her shoulder. She ran her hands along the firm muscles on his thighs. "At least we're on the same wavelength."

"Good, I'd really hate to think you didn't want me to join in," Ty purred next to her ear.

"Active participation is definitely encouraged."

Ty chuckled at her breathless comeback. He nipped at the soft spot between her shoulder and her neck then slid his hands to her waist. "Bend over, baby."

Evan placed her hands on the headboard. She cast Ty a seductive smile over her shoulder before she used her hold on the headboard to allow her to bend over as far as she could.

"Inventive."

She smiled at the admiration in Ty's tone as she tightened her grip on the headboard and flexed her inner walls around his erection. "Just trusting this will be an experience I won't soon forget."

Ty palmed her hips and growled low in his throat when her walls contracted around him again. "Easy, sweetheart. Give me a chance to move."

Evan pushed back against him, forcing his cock deeper inside her. She moaned at the satisfying sensation. "Then by all means..."

Ty withdrew then slowly slid back inside her.

Evan clenched her jaw at her body's reaction to the unique position. Chill bumps formed on her skin.

He pulled out and pushed back in once more. When he began to rock while he was partway inside her, Evan's arms and legs started to tremble at the pleasure his movements caused. "God, Ty. I'm...I mean...that feels so good."

"I want you to feel even more," he said as he flattened the palm of his hand against her lower belly. Ty pushed toward her spine at the same time he thrust forcefully inside her again and again. Evan realized the reason he wasn't ramming deep. Ty knew the position allowed his cock to hit her hot spot with just the right friction. When Ty's fingers brushed against her clitoris, Evan let out a long mewling wail.

Her orgasm raced through her in a series of rapidly building jolts of pleasure. The pressure from his hand only intensified the body-rocking sensations clamoring inside her. Her belly knotted, her heart raced and her body tensed as her climax built to its highest peak. The ecstasy that splintered within her made her gasp at the intensity. Evan clenched her walls and rocked into him as her orgasm spiraled its way throughout her entire body.

When the last contraction subsided, Evan pulled herself up to an upright position and used her hold on the bed as leverage to push back against each of Ty's aggressive thrusts. This time she clenched her muscles, making it more difficult for him to withdraw.

Ty stopped moving for a second and laid his head on her shoulder. His breath came in harsh bellows. "God you've got a helluva grip, baby. Give a little."

Evan grinned as she let go of her pelvic muscles then quickly gripped him once more. Ty shuddered against her back. When she finally relaxed her channel, Ty gripped her hips and pulled his erection completely out of her, then slammed back inside her again and again. "Tyyyyyy," she cried out. The hard pressure sent her right over the edge into a second, deeply satisfying climax.

"You feel so damn good." Ty gripped her breasts and held her back tight against his chest as he ground his hips against her rear. He was so deep inside her that when he came, Evan felt each explosive pulse. The intimate sensation sent warmth tingling throughout the rest of her body.

Ty's movements slowed until his body was flush with hers. Heat emanated between them as he slid his right hand under her left breast. Without a word he tucked his hand right up against her thundering heart. Using his hold, he pulled her tight and kissed a path along her neck until he reached her ear. "Whose heart do you think is beating faster?"

Evan felt the heavy thud of his heart hammering against her back. She closed her eyes and placed her hand over his on her heart. She took a steadying breath. "They're beating at the same jackhammer rate."

The low, sexy growl next to her ear sent a thrilling shiver down her spine, but his next words blew her away. "That's because we're evenly matched."

Chapter Eight

Evan sat in her chair watching Ty walk a radiant Jena down the aisle between the rows of white chairs with purple flowers and white bows tied to the "aisle" side. Her father sat to her right and Ty's mother and uncle sat to her left. She felt very self-conscious when Ty introduced her to his mom as the town's veterinarian, especially since Lily chose that moment to walk past them in her perfectly tailored navy suit and her silky black hair pulled up in a French twist. Not a single wisp escaped.

Lily was the epitome of sophistication. The woman oozed confidence with every step she took. Evan had plucked nervously at the skirt of her simple lavender rayon sundress while Ty introduced her to his mother. She'd resisted the urge to wipe her sweaty palm on her dress before she put her hand out shake Karen Hudson's hand. But Ty's mother just smiled and shook her hand as if she'd never been happier to meet her.

Karen's green eyes and short dark hair favored Ty's overall coloring, but Evan could see where Jena inherited her mother's friendly nature. When Mrs. Hudson asked Evan and her father to sit next to her and her brother-in-law during the wedding, Evan quickly came to the conclusion Mrs. Hudson was a gracious and generous woman.

Evan's gaze locked on Ty's handsome form as he handed his sister off to his Uncle Rick and then moved to stand behind Harm's best man.

When the pastor began the wedding ceremony, Evan's gaze remained on Ty. He looked so incredibly handsome in his expensive black business suit, she'd had a hard time keeping her hands to herself when he got dressed for the wedding. On the way to Harm's ranch, Ty told her his sister had insisted on no tuxedos for the groomsmen since Harm and she were marrying outside and they wanted the wedding to be a fun, informal affair.

Ty's broad shoulders filled out his suit to perfection and his starched white shirt made his skin look even darker. He'd really picked up a nice tan during his short stay in Boone, she thought with a half-jealous smirk as she glanced at her bare arms' peachy skin tone. Her skin never turned dark. Instead, it only turned a golden color when she worked outside for extended periods of time.

Evan took a quick glance back through the three-hundred-plus guests who were in attendance at the wedding. Her gaze caught Chad's across the aisle and diagonally back a few rows. Or his caught hers, rather.

Chad tilted his cowboy hat her way as a big, broad grin spread across his face.

He pointed to her and then himself and winked as he mouthed, "Dance."

Evan turned around without acknowledging him. Damn, she'd forgotten she'd told him she'd dance with him at the wedding reception. She bit her lip, wondering how she was going to get out of that. If Chad danced like a normal man she wouldn't have an issue. But Chad always danced close while his hands did a dance all their own. If Ty saw that… She grimaced at the thought of being the cause of another scene. The good news was there were a lot of guests at this wedding. Since she wore flats, she should be able to get lost in the general crowd pretty easily.

She happened to look at Ty at that moment and that's when she saw Ty's gaze had zeroed in on Chad. Though his expression remained impassive, Evan could tell by the direct look in his eyes, he was challenging Chad. As much as the possessive look in Ty's eyes made her heart sing when he cast his gaze her way before returning to Chad's, it also made her stomach tense.

She took a breath and vowed to find a way to avoid Chad until Ty was finished with his groomsman duties.

* * * * *

Evan grabbed a glass of wine off a table before she ducked behind a huge potted plant the florist had brought in to decorate—in other words, hide—each of the huge white tent's four corner posts. Taking a sip, Evan swallowed and took a deep breath while she leaned against the pole. Dodging Chad for the last half-hour had taken a lot of physical dexterity and effort on her part. Damn, she was exhausted.

"Evan, love, there you are," Chad called out as he rounded the other side of the plant. "Remember, you promised—"

"Okaaaaay, let's open a space on the dance floor, everyone. Now's the time for all the bachelors to gather together. Harm's going to throw the garter," Mrs. Hudson's voice came through the mic as the song ended.

Relief washed over Evan at the interruption. She grinned at Chad. "Better get going, Chad. You're still single."

Chad waved her comment away, but at that moment Jena called out from the stage, "You, too, Chad."

Everyone turned and called his name. "C'mon, Chad, m'boy. Get up there," his father bellowed from across the tent.

Chad thrived on attention, especially large crowds. He gave the whole group a huge smile and waved to them as he walked away from Evan to join the single men who'd gathered on the dance floor near the stage.

Harm was up on the stage on bent knee in front of his new wife. A huge grin spread across his face at the catcalls that went on as he grasped his wife's ankle under her long wedding gown before he slowly slid his hands up her leg, seeking the garter.

When his hand went well past her knee, he tilted his head in surprise and asked, "How far up does this garter go, darlin'?"

The crowd all laughed at his comment while Jena grinned and bent forward to whisper something in his ear.

"Now that she's got me all hot and bothered she tells me it's on the other leg," Harm mock-complained to the crowd. Among uproarious laughter and even more catcalling, Harm moved his hands to Jena's other leg, shaking his head at his wife's sense of humor.

Conversation buzzed around her as Evan watched Harm remove Jena's garter. When he stood up and held his prize aloft on one finger, Evan immediately looked for Ty. Was he among the men who waited to catch the garter?

When she saw him on the fringes of the group of men, as if he only stood there because he had to since he was a groomsman, she couldn't help but feel a bit disappointed. She knew what tradition said the garter symbolically meant...the one who caught the garter would marry next. Is that why Ty didn't seem to want to join in?

Harm turned his back to the crowd and tossed the garter over his head. The garter sailed through the air until one very determined male hand reached out above all others and grasped the blue and white material in a tight fist. Chad came down from his jump in the air with a triumphant smile on his face.

As she watched the other single men clap Chad on the back in congratulations, Evan let out a breath of thanks. Good. Chad would be busy for a little while at least.

Her neck tingled and she instinctively knew she was being watched. Evan turned to see Ty standing beside her.

"Hey."

The intensity in his gaze as it slowly moved down her body then back to her face took her breath away.

"Hey yourself." She took a sip of her wine and tried to act nonchalant. Ty didn't need to know just how much he affected her. No one who was leaving tomorrow should affect her this much, damn it.

Ty reached up and cupped the back of her neck. Her stomach tumbled when he rubbed his thumb along her jaw line.

"I'm sorry I haven't been around."

She smiled. "I understand it's the groomsman's duty to 'work' the party."

Ty gave her a sexy smile. "I'll do my best to make sure at least one guest has a great time." He began to pull her closer when his mother's voice came across the mic once more.

"Okay, all you single ladies. Now it's your turn to grab for the golden ring…well, in this case Jena's bouquet. Come on. Gather around."

Ty wrapped his arm around Evan and kissed her temple before he gave her a push. "Get going, sassy. There's a bouquet with your name on it."

As Evan walked away, she grinned at Ty over her shoulder. "For once my height just might come in handy."

Ty winked and called after her, "Elbow throwing is illegal."

"I'll keep that in mind." Evan felt on top of the world. Just those few moments alone with Ty put a bounce in her step as she made her way to stand among the group of single women waiting for Jena to throw her bouquet.

"I heard Jena's right-handed, so my guess is since she'll be throwing over her head to us the flowers will go toward the left."

Evan shook her head at the two dark-haired ladies in their early thirties who stood in front of her discussing their tactics. They had their plans of capturing the bouquet down to a science.

Harm stood behind Jena as she waved to the group of women. "Hi, ladies. Are you ready?"

"Yes!" everyone called in unison.

Evan didn't plan to get involved in the fun but everyone's enthusiasm around her was so infectious. She called out "yes" along with everyone else as her heart rate picked up in excitement.

Jena smiled and turned her back to the crowd. "One, two, three," she said right before she launched the bouquet over her head.

The purple and white floral bouquet made a high arc in the air before it zoomed straight down into Evan's hands.

Evan stood there dumbfounded as the crowd applauded and called out, "Evan, Evan, Evan!"

She even laughed when she heard a loud, "Yeehaw!" But her laughter turned into a gasp of surprise when Chad barreled through the crowd yelling, "Evan's next to get hitched and so am I." At the same time he grasped her around the waist. Throwing her over his shoulder, Chad played right into the uproarious laughter around them. "Guess we'd better have our fun while we can. Right, folks?"

Everyone laughed and more than a few men yelled out, "Hell yeah!"

"Very funny," Evan mumbled from her upside-down position facing Chad's back.

When Chad headed off the dance floor and straight toward the edge of the tent, apprehension made her stomach tense.

"You can let me down now," she said in as low a voice as she could.

Ty narrowed his eyes as he watched the bullshit excuse Chad concocted to capture Evan's attention. The prick knew she wouldn't cause a scene in what appeared to be a good-natured joke. But Ty saw the way Chad's arm tightened around Evan's thighs when he walked off the dance floor. As the arrogant cowboy headed to the side of Harm's ranch home as if he planned to continue toward the front, Ty felt a tight pain in his chest. When Chad's hand cupped Evan's ass right as he turned out of sight, Ty clenched his jaw.

Ty had taken all of five steps when a heavy hand landed on his arm.

"I don't want to have to arrest anyone today."

Ty cut his sharp gaze to the person who dared stop his exit and was surprised to stare into Sheriff Master's intense gaze.

"Am I clear?"

Ty gave the sheriff a curt nod. "Perfectly."

As soon as Jake let go of Ty's arm, Chad came barreling around the side of the house riding a horse. Evan sat across his lap. Her legs dangled down the horse's left side as she grasped Chad's shoulders tight.

"Yeeeeehaw!" Chad yelled as the horse thundered toward them. The crowd clapped and laughed at his antics.

Ty cast a murderous gaze the sheriff's way. Before he could speak, something hit him on the side of his head as the horse pounded past them.

Ty's heart jerked at the impact, but he recovered and captured the assault weapon before it fell to the ground. He was holding Jena's bouquet.

"Hold that for me!" Evan called out.

Ty's gaze locked with Evan's annoyed one as she shifted her gaze to Chad and rolled her eyes.

Biting, possessive anger, unlike anything Ty had ever experienced in his life, spread through him like wildfire. He turned and started to walk toward the side of the house, his shoulders and back tense, already mentally preparing to defend his woman.

"Hold up, son."

Ty stopped walking, ready to explode if the sheriff tried to tell him to stay out of it. He cast his gaze back toward the imposing man.

Jake's stare narrowed on Chad's retreating back as the horse took off toward the open pastures behind Harm's home. "I'll bet with your skills you can do some damage without any physical evidence, can't you?"

Ty's tense shoulders relaxed. He gave the sheriff a broad, deadly smile. "Only in defense."

The sheriff squinted after the horse and flicked his tongue over his teeth. Fatherly protection emanated from him as he crossed his arms. "Looks to me like my daughter needs some defendin'."

* * * * *

Once they were out of sight, Chad slowed the stolen horse to a trot.

Evan scowled up at Chad. "Very funny. You can take me back now."

Chad's arm tightened around her waist. "No can do, honey." He glanced down at her for a second. "You owe me a dance, remember?"

She was already annoyed with Chad for absconding with one of Harm's horses. The horse was saddled and tied up in the stables. It had streamers of purple and white ribbons tied to the saddle horn for a reason. Chad was starting to piss her off.

"Fine. But the music and the dance floor are back under the tent."

"Where you'll try to avoid me the rest of the wedding." He shook his head. "Nuh-uh, woman. You promised me a dance." He lowered his head and nuzzled her neck. "I guess I'll just have to sing to you for the background music."

"And just how do you expect me to dance with you while I have my hands clapped over my ears?"

Chad smirked at her insult as he stopped the horse. "Nice try, but you're not getting out of it." When he finished speaking, he moved his legs back a little and set her on the saddle. Evan gripped the top of saddle horn and prayed the horse didn't move while Chad jumped down or she'd be kissing the grass.

Chad grabbed her waist before she had a chance to turn and sit astride. She'd have done so, even in her dress, just to get back to the wedding. Evan ground her teeth and placed her hands on Chad's shoulders to steady herself while he lifted her down. Once her feet hit the ground, she let go and took a step back. "I know what you're really after, Chad. You may as well give up, because it isn't going to happen."

Chad grabbed her around the waist and yanked her close. "Why? Is it because of that Yank? I understand he'll be leaving tomorrow. But I'll always be here, Evan. Boone is our home." His grip tightened on her waist as his mouth lowered to hers.

Chad had deliberately made her face facts. Ty would leave tomorrow. Gone. Back to his home and his business in Maryland, and all she'd be left with was memories of their time together. She'd never been so angry in her life.

She tried to shove Chad back, but he grasped her shoulders and planted his lips over hers in a hard kiss.

Evan felt nothing, absolutely nothing when Chad tried to deepen the kiss. Other than anger. That emotion definitely ran rampant through her mind. She pulled her mouth away from his and whacked him in the nose. Hard.

"Ow!" Chad yelled as he backed up and held his hands to his nose. Then he turned his blood-streaked palm toward her. "Shit! I think you just broke my nose."

Evan crossed her arms over her chest. "That'll teach to take 'no' as a 'no'."

His eyes widened in disbelief as he covered his nose once more. "But you didn't say 'no'."

"Oh, so me trying to shove you back was a 'yes' in your book?"

"No. I mean…yes. Hell, woman, you're trying to confuse me."

"Lean forward."

"Huh?"

Evan turned at the sound of a horse's hoofbeats approaching fast. "I said, lean forward. Don't tilt your head back or you might swallow the blood. Pinch your nose, too. It'll stop the bleeding faster." Her heart leapt at the sight of Ty galloping toward them on the back of one of Harm's horses. The man leaned into the horse like he'd been born in the saddle. He'd ditched his jacket and tie and had unbuttoned his collared shirt, but in her mind, nothing was sexier than seeing Ty riding in to save her in his wedding garb and a huge purple and white floral wreath swaying around the horse's neck. The sight of the flowers made her stomach tense. Those purple and white ribbons on the horse Chad stole definitely had a purpose.

The ground shook beneath her feet until Ty stopped his horse a few feet away.

"Need a ride, ma'am?" he asked.

She noted the smirk of amusement that lit in Ty's green gaze when he glanced at Chad and saw the man's predicament.

Evan walked over and put her hand in Ty's outstretched one. As he helped her up to sit sideways on the saddle in front of him, Chad called out in a nasal voice as he continued to pinch his nose, "I can take Evan back."

Ty wrapped his arms around Evan's waist and nudged his horse forward until they stood beside the horse Chad had taken.

Leaning over, he grabbed the other horse's reins and started to turn both horses around.

"Wait! You can't leave me here. I need a ride back."

Evan felt Ty's body tense behind her. "I'm taking both horses. They were waiting to be Harm and Jena's ride away from their wedding reception."

"Oh no," Evan whispered at Ty's confirmation of her concerns about the decorated saddle horn on the horse Chad took. Chad might've been the one who stole the horse, but she couldn't help the embarrassed heat that rode her cheeks as Ty began to trot away with the horses.

When they reached the stables, Ty's arm tightened around Evan's waist and his lips moved close to her ear. "I want to know why you didn't tell me you were a vet."

Evan turned to look up at him. "Only if you tell me—"

Ty's lips landed on hers, heated and demanding.

Her heart raced at the intensity of his kiss. Evan reached up and touched his jaw. She opened her mouth under his, wishing they were alone for more than a brief few minutes. She had a feeling someone would come looking for them soon.

Ty pulled his mouth away and stared down into her eyes, waiting for her to answer.

Evan returned his heart-stopping stare. For several seconds her pulse pounded in her ears. Did she really want to open up to Ty? To tell him one of her biggest insecurities. His hand moved from her waist to her thigh and squeezed. Not a word was spoken, but she realized from that one touch her trust seemed very important to him.

Evan started to speak when a familiar booming voice interrupted her.

"Evelyn! There you are."

Her father walked up to the horse and put his hands in the air to help her down. Evan cast an apologetic look Ty's way before she put her hands on her father's shoulders and allowed him to lower her to the ground.

"Hey, Dad."

Her father looked up at Ty as he put his arm around her shoulders. "No arrests?"

Ty shook his head.

"What are you two talking about?" Evan asked as her father steered her out of the stables and back toward the festivities.

Jake chuckled. "Nothing. Just men-speak."

As Ty watched Evan walk away with her father, he couldn't help but feel frustrated. Evan was the most independent woman he'd ever met. Despite the fact her father was the town sheriff and overprotective to boot, he had a feeling she'd skipped the crawling stage and went straight to walking on her own two feet just as soon as her legs would hold her weight.

He should be relieved he didn't have to kick the shit out of Chad—everything his aikido training had ingrained in him focused on self-defense only, that he should never take the aggressive offensive. But he wasn't relieved. Instead, seeing the evidence Evan had taken care of herself caused his male pride to take a hit. Frustration built inside him like a storm brewing to full throttle fury. Why he felt this way, he didn't have a fucking clue. All he knew was he wanted to see Evan's vulnerable side. Hell, he wanted to know she had one. If nothing else, he wanted her to trust him enough to tell why she'd lied to him.

He climbed off his horse and retied both horses' reins back to their posts to await the bride and groom.

* * * * *

Ty clasped Evan's hand tight and tugged her up the stairs and into the Double D ranch house. She followed him, unsure of his quiet mood. After she'd walked away with her father from the stables, Ty had had more wedding duties to fulfill, so they didn't see each other again until Harm and Jena rode off at the end of the wedding reception.

"Ty, what is it?" She tried to get a response from him, but he remained stoic.

He tossed his jacket on the back of the couch and then tugged her into the bathroom with him, shutting the door behind him. Evan pulled out of his hold, her chest tightening in apprehension. "What's wrong?"

Ty flipped on the shower then turned her around. When he unzipped the back of her dress then moved his fingers to the straps on her shoulders, Evan held onto the scraps of material before he could pull them down her arms.

She cast a serious gaze over her shoulder. "Talk to me, damn it, or these clothes aren't coming off."

Ty's hooded gaze remained on hers as he let go of her straps and began to unbutton his own shirt. Evan couldn't resist. She turned to face him while he shrugged out of the cotton shirt. Broad, tan shoulders, a mouthwatering chest and cut abs she'd never get tired of seeing surfaced as his shirt landed in a heap on the floor. Evan had to press her lips together to keep the anger she felt in the forefront of her mind.

Heat began to fill the room. Steam hung in the air around them like a physical manifestation of the sexual tension that vibrated between them.

Ty's fingers moved to her straps once more. Evan's breathing turned shallow. The man literally made her achy and breathless and he'd yet to touch her. She was so caught up in his deep green gaze she let her hands fall to her sides.

When her dress slid down her body to pool at her feet, Ty's line of sight lowered to her bare breasts as he pulled the bowstring untying one side of her underwear, then the other.

Evan's gaze followed the filmy black material until it fluttered to land on top of her dress. She realized that underwear was the only sexy piece of underclothing she owned. She'd have to remedy that sad situation. Her heart raced at the sight of Ty's fingers lightly brushing the strawberry-blonde curls between her legs.

He hooked a finger under her chin and applied pressure until her gaze met his once more. "You trust me to take away your clothes—a physical protection of your body. I want you to trust me enough in your heart to tell me the truth."

Evan's chest lurched at Ty's words. Each time they were together, the man dug a little deeper into her heart. She knew if she opened up to him it would hurt so much more when he left, but she'd never felt so close to another. It just felt right to share with this incredible, complex man, but she'd do it her way.

She smiled as she unbuckled his belt and then unbuttoned and unzipped his dress pants. "You sure know how to get right to the heart of things, don't you?"

As she hooked her thumbs on the waistband of his boxers, a warning tone entered Ty's voice, "Evan."

Evan pushed his boxers down his thighs, kissing her way down his abdomen.

Ty's stomach muscles flexed underneath her lips. His fingers shot through her hair when she let his boxers fall the rest of the way down to his ankles as she blew her hot breath across his erection's sensitive skin.

"Evan, stop trying to distract me."

Evan smiled at the tension in his tone, then ran her tongue from the base of his erection all the way to the tip in a slow, leisurely lick. "There's no distraction going on, Ty. Just a two-way street." She straightened and faced him square-on. "I don't plan on venturing down it alone."

Ty's fingers curled in her scalp, his touch tense, possessive...affected. He pulled her flush against his body, his lips a breath away from hers. Her stomach tightened at the exhilarating sensation of his hard cock pressed against her lower belly and the coiled tension in his muscular arms around her.

"Why do you always challenge me?"

The mix of emotions churning in his eyes surprised her. Evan stood on her toes and kissed his mouth full-on. "Because you need it."

The truth of Evan's words pierced right to his heart, making his chest constrict. Not only did he have to have the sexual attraction, but he needed the stimulating banter. He wanted a woman who gave as good as she got, but deep in his heart he also knew he needed a woman who gave him as high a priority as he did her. Lily had definitely left her mark on him. She'd taught him what he didn't want in a woman.

Ty lifted Evan in his arms and stepped under the warm, hard shower spray. Setting her on her feet, he grasped her upper back and lowered his mouth to her breast, capturing the nipple.

He sucked hard on the sensitive nub until Evan's fingers tightened in his hair.

She arched her back and moaned, clutching him closer. Ty nipped at the pink tip and moved his hands lower to clasp her sweet rear.

The sensation of the water sluicing over them and her soft skin rubbing against his erection made his cock throb to be inside her as soon as possible.

He kissed his way to her other breast and applied the same attention. "Tell me, Evan," he mumbled before he rolled her nipple between his teeth.

Evan's breath came out in short, rapid pants as her fingers grasped the muscles along his hips. "Not…fair."

Ty slid his hand down her belly to her mound while he rubbed his five o'clock shadow across her nipple, swollen from his kisses. "Who said I was a fair man?"

Evan grabbed his balls. He shuddered at her touch and the fact her aggression turned him on even more.

She slowly trailed her fingers up his cock. "All's fair…" she shot back.

He chuckled at her moxie. The woman yanked his chain better than any female he'd ever been with.

"My IQ ranges from 140 to 155 depending on what IQ test I've been given."

Ty met her gaze, surprised by her statement. Before he could speak, she continued, "I went to college when I was sixteen and had my vet's license and MBA by time I turned twenty-four." She grimaced. "Let's just say, growing up the sheriff's daughter, combined with the ability to spin intellectual circles around men, was a deadly combination in the relationship department."

"Translated…it's a huge turnoff."

"Yep, except to Chad, apparently." She shrugged. "From past experience…well, that's why I lied."

Ty gathered her close and buried his nose in her neck. "Baby, your ability to improvise and adapt has impressed me both intellectually and sexually, and I'm sure as hell not intimidated by your dad."

Evan laughed as she stroked his broad shoulders. "I definitely think we're on the same page in the pleasure department."

"But there's one thing…"

She raised her eyebrows and held her breath, waiting for him to continue.

"You've worked hard for your doctorate. You deserve the respect you've earned. Don't be afraid to ask for it because you started off younger than your peers."

Her stomach tensed at his comment. "What are you taking about? My patients respect my judgment."

Ty shook his head and gave her a half-smile. "I can tell they respect you, but have you noticed none of them call you Doctor Masters?"

Evan laughed his comment off. She had noticed, but gave up worrying about it. "That's because they've all known me since I was a kid. They saw me hanging around Doc Peterson's veterinary office all the time, watching him do his job. He retired the year I got my vet's license." She smiled at the memory. "Said he was just waiting on me to finish up my schoolin' so he could leave his animals in good hands."

Ty's dark eyebrows drew downward as if he knew she was trying to downplay his comment. "You've earned the title, Evan."

Evan grinned and began to tickle his waist. "And *you* need to loosen up and laugh a lot more."

Ty grabbed her hands and held them captive. "Stop that."

The warm water beat down on them and then bounced off their shoulders in tiny spatters as she met his serious gaze.

"Why? Because you'll laugh? What's wrong with being silly?" she asked as she began to slide her slippery foot up his leg.

Ty's lips twitched as if he were trying not to fall victim to her antics.

Evan grinned. "Oooh, I think he's about to laugh. As a matter of fact, I predict a deep-bellied guffaw coming."

Ty laughed outright and then gave her a brilliant smile. It was the kind of smile that was so engaging, it startled Evan. The man might be handsome as hell with his intense, brooding persona, but he damn near bowled her over when he turned on the charm. Her breath literally caught in her chest at the sight of the first truly genuine happy-go-lucky smile she'd seen since she met him. Evan cleared her throat to cover her surprise. "Now it's your turn."

He raised a dark eyebrow. "My turn?"

"To share."

Ty nodded and pulled her close until she laid her head on his shoulder. "When I was seventeen I fell in love. The girl was the first woman I had sex with. I was her first as well." He took a deep breath, remembering the pain Lily's words had caused. "Let's just say, after a whole summer together, she didn't think I was the man for her."

Evan's chest tightened at the heartbreak she heard in Ty's voice. She wrapped her arms around his trim waist and hugged him tight. "Was Lily that woman?" she asked in a quiet voice.

Ty's body tensed for a second before he cupped the back of her head and ran his fingers down her wet hair. "Yeah. She thought pursuing her professional aspirations was more important than us, that I would only hold her back."

The tone of his voice made Evan's stomach tense. No wonder he had a thing against sleeping with virgins. It wasn't what he'd originally told her—that he thought the woman would expect some kind of commitment from the act, but that *he* had thought being Lily's first had meant more in their relationship. In the end, Lily had chewed him up and spit him out.

Evan had heard her girlfriends talk about their first love…that they'd never forget them. She knew she'd never forget Ty. What had started out as a convenient means to an end had turned into so much more. She realized she'd fallen in love with this deeply intense, fiercely protective yet surprisingly tender man. She'd never forget their time together. Ever.

She took a deep breath. Her heart ached, but she had to know how Ty felt about Lily after all this time. "Do you still love her?"

Ty stopped stroking her hair. A long heart-stopping moment passed before he answered.

"No."

Relief spread through her. She slowly exhaled the breath she'd been holding.

Tension filled the air between them. She didn't want Ty's last night in Texas to be filled with sad thoughts. She wanted him to stay, but he hadn't said anything to indicate he felt deeper feelings for her beyond their physical attraction. Plus, he had a business to run back in Maryland. The least she could do, as a thank you to Ty for fulfilling her request, was to send the man off with happier memories of Boone.

Picking up the bar of soap, she cast him a wicked grin. "You know, ever since I saw you in the shower the other day, I've been dying for a repeat performance. Only this time, I want to stay until the climactic ending."

Ty flashed her a rakish grin as he took the soap and ran it along her palm. Her heart thundered and her lower belly tensed in sexual excitement as he set the soap back on the dish then guided her hand to his erection. He slowly wrapped her soapy fingers around his cock.

Bending close, he kissed her neck at the same time he cupped her mound in a dominant, possessive hold. As he slid a finger deep in her channel, the low, rumbling register of his voice sent intense excitement straight to her toes. "How about this time we're both intimately involved in the pleasurable finale."

* * * * *

The sensation of someone's lips pressed against her temple woke Evan. Ty's soap and masculine scent surrounded her. She inhaled, then stretched and smiled.

"Morning, Doc."

Her eyes flew open at the nickname Ty had used. She knew he meant it as a compliment. When her morning eyes focused on his clean-shaven face and damp hair, Evan's heart jerked. It was Sunday. She knew he was leaving at some point today. She sat up on her elbow and took in his dark heather-green T-shirt and faded blue jeans.

"Where are you going, good-lookin'?" She tried her best to sound as casual as possible even though her heart was already breaking into tiny pieces.

Ty ran his hand down her hair and cupped her chin. She liked the tiny lines that formed around his eyes when he smiled. They told her what she already knew. Ty smiled more often than he let on. "My mom wanted me to join my uncle and her for breakfast with Harm and Jena before the newlyweds left for their honeymoon."

Relief flooded through her, relaxing the tension that had stiffened her shoulders. Yesterday, after their shower and a quick dinner, Ty had carried her to bed and kept her up until the wee hours, taking her to new sexual highs. Her body might ache in a bone-deep I-couldn't-get-enough-of-this-man-so-I'm-going-to-pay-for-it-later kind of way, but she'd never regret one single moment she'd spent with Ty.

"What time is your flight?"

"Two." Ty leaned forward and brushed his lips against hers before he whispered in her ear, "The well-tumbled look suits you."

Heat rose to her cheeks when Ty's intense gaze met hers once more.

"Damn, I wish I hadn't promised I'd meet my family for breakfast."

She grinned then lay down on her back and stretched like a languorous cat, pressing her naked breasts against the thin sheet covering her body. "I guess I'll just lounge around in bed all day then."

"Don't tempt me," Ty growled as he stood. He glanced at his watch. "It's nine now. I should be back in an hour and a half. Will you still be here?"

Evan laughed and answered truthfully. "Yes, recovering."

Ty chuckled and started to leave the bedroom. But he turned back, a quizzical expression on his face. "I'm curious. You're obviously an animal lover, but since you've spent a few days here I have to assume you don't have any pets at home to take care of. Why don't you?"

Evan leaned up on her elbow, surprised by his question about her personal life beyond what he already knew. "As you know I'm pretty much on call all the time. It wouldn't be fair to have a pet I don't get to spend much time with. And my yard is very small. I'd want to have more land for my pets." She gave him a half-smile and shrugged. "One day. For now, I look at it this way...I have a whole practice full of pets."

Ty nodded his understanding to her answer before he turned and left the bedroom.

Evan listened to the sound of Ty's shoes on the wooden floor until he'd walked out of the house and started his car.

Once he'd driven away, she got out of bed and stretched every protesting muscle in her body. *A shower...that's what I need. The heat will help loosen my muscles.* She headed for the bathroom whistling an uplifting tune.

She had at least an hour with Ty before he had to leave. When he got back, she wasn't going to dwell on the leaving part, but enjoy every last minute of the here-and-now part.

* * * * *

Ty's mind shifted through thoughts in rapid succession as he turned his car and headed up the dirt road that led to the Double D ranch. He'd never felt so free and excited in all his thirty-six years, all because of a woman who knew how to enjoy life to its fullest, a woman whom he was drawn to both intellectually and physically—a woman he just couldn't get enough of. Evan was everything he wanted…everything that mattered. She was dedicated, generous, sassy and …independent.

That last descriptive word struck him hard. Evan was incredibly self-sufficient. Would she want someone like him in her life—a man with a protective streak a mile wide—for more than a weekend? For that matter, what *did* he want from this? He'd never expected the young veterinarian to turn his heart inside out, that having mind-blowing sex with Evan would meld into making love. But that's what he'd done last night. Even if she wasn't aware, he'd made love to Evan. Did she feel it?

He didn't want to open his heart up again, to leave himself vulnerable for the kind of heartbreak that took him at least a decade to overcome. His feelings for Evan ran so much deeper than they had for Lily. Lily didn't make him shudder when her fingers grazed his skin. He'd laughed a lot back then, but Lily didn't try to see beyond his laughter to his insecurities. She didn't look that deep.

Evan bowled right through his carefully erected emotional barriers. With her infectious smile and upbeat personality, she made him look at himself, see he was being an ass and showed him how to laugh again. He'd forgotten what it was like to laugh so freely with another…hell, come to think of it, he hadn't allowed himself the luxury in eighteen years.

But he had to face facts. He lived in Maryland and she lived in Texas. What did the future hold for them?

The sight of Evan's SUV coming toward him, dirt kicking up behind her tires, drew him out of his reverie. Ty glanced at his watch to make sure he hadn't somehow run late. No. He was right on time.

He pulled his car over and put on his brakes at the same time Evan did the same.

"Hey, I saw you left your cell phone behind, so I tried to call Jena, but you'd already left their house. I've got an emergency surgery at my office."

Ty couldn't help the sinking feeling that knotted his stomach. He adopted a neutral expression. "How long do you think you'll be?"

Evan's ponytail swished behind her as she shook her head. "I don't know. The cat's pretty mangled from what I understand." She gave him an apologetic smile. "I'm sorry, Ty. I'll call your cell when I get a better idea of the situation, okay?"

Ty clamped his jaw to keep from blurting out, "But I want you to stay, damn it." He knew it was a selfish reaction…one he couldn't help thinking.

"Good luck with the cat." He gave her a firm nod, then put his foot on the gas pedal and headed toward the house.

* * * * *

Evan called Ty's cell phone on her way back to the Double D. Tears streamed down her cheeks, her emotions at an all-time high as her vehicle's wheels rumbled over the potholes in the dirt road. After spending a couple of hours trying to repair the damage to the cat, she lost the poor soul anyway. It was the first animal she'd lost during a surgery. The sad experience coupled with the fact she'd never been able to call Ty to say goodbye made her reaction that much stronger.

When the house came into view and she saw Ty's car was gone, she couldn't hold back the sob that escaped. In her heart, she'd hoped Ty had changed his flight to stay longer so they could say a proper goodbye. His empty parking space told her otherwise.

She'd parked and cut the engine by the time Ty's voicemail came on. Evan closed her eyes and listened to his deep voice, her heart aching.

As the beep sounded, she sniffed back her tears and adopted a steady tone. Ty didn't need to know how upset she was.

"Ty, I'm so sorry I wasn't able to call you before you left. The surgery…" she paused and took a steadying breath, "it took longer than I anticipated. I wish I'd had a chance to say goodbye. Well, I guess that's what I'm doing now, though I'm finding it hard to come up with the words while speaking to your voicemail. Call me."

Evan punched the off button and climbed out of her car. Butterflies flitted in her belly and her hopes picked up at the thought Ty might have left her a note. She shut the car door and strode over to the porch, taking the steps two at a time in her haste to get inside.

She unlocked the door and opened it, her gaze instantly searching places Ty might have left her a note in the small house.

The sight of a white sheet of paper sitting on the kitchen table made her heart race. Her boot heels sounded loud in the empty house as she walked over and picked up the note Ty had left her.

Evan,

You know that vet's assistant you pretended to be…have you considered the possibility you might need one.

Ty

Evan's heart felt as if someone squeezed it with all their might. The pain was so great her breath came in rampant pants. The note slid out of her fingers and fluttered to the floor as she plopped in one of the chairs, unable to stand on her suddenly shaky legs. Not one word of goodbye. No "I had a good time. Take care". Nothing. Just a curt note, written not in a question form, but as a statement—a statement that basically said she wasn't capable of handling her practice on her own.

Deep hurt welled within her.

Chapter Nine

Evan stood in front of the black glass-front cabinet in one of her exam rooms. Clipboard and pen in hand, she'd already checked the other exam rooms' supplies. She could've had her secretary do this task, but she wanted to be absolutely certain all the exam rooms were stocked with all necessary supplies.

It'd been four weeks since Ty had left without a word. He never had returned her phone call. It took her a week and a half to overcome the hurt Ty's silence had caused. That's when the realization hit her. Could it be that Ty thought she was just like Lily? A woman who cared only for her own self, who put her desires above all else?

No matter how hurt she was by the way Ty left, his comment in the note he'd left behind had stuck with her. Evan didn't realize she'd allowed her job to become her life the past few years, but the truth was, because of the way she'd grown up—smarter and younger than her peers—she never really did fit in. As the town's vet, she felt as if she truly belonged and was accepted for who she was. So she'd thrown herself into her career without taking time out for herself. In the past, it didn't matter…she didn't have anyone else in her life. Until she met Ty.

She checked the inventory items off her list and wondered what Ty was doing now. Thoughts of him still made her heart ache.

"See you on Monday, Doctor Masters. I've got Doc Peterson's number written down if I need him," Nicole called out from the front office.

"Evening, Nicole…and it's Evan," Evan called back with a sigh. The new vet assistant Nicole Shannon she'd hired a couple of weeks ago had insisted on calling her Doctor Masters from day one. Marlene, her secretary, had even joined in this new campaign to the point several of her patients this past week had started calling her Doc Masters. *Wouldn't Ty be pleased?* she thought with an ironic twist of her lips as she set the clipboard down on the counter and finished checking off her list.

Something dropped on the clipboard then bounced to the floor at her feet.

Evan pulled at her prairie skirt to move the calf-length hem so she could see what had fallen. Her brow furrowed at the sight of the blue and white garter that had landed between her beige boots. She'd seen Chad driving around in his brand-new convertible with that damn garter hanging from his mirror. The couple of times he'd seen her, he'd flicked the garter and raised his eyebrows as if to say it was only a matter of time before he'd get her to go out with him again. She really wasn't in the mood for his games today.

"Chad—"

She tensed at the sound of his boots stepping into her personal space and then froze when he pressed his chest against her back.

Masculine hands landed on the counter on either side of her, caging her in. They weren't Chad's.

"I have this ache that needs tending to and there's only one doctor I want to do the job."

Ty's deep voice made her heart rate kick up while his masculine scent and body heat enveloped her in a blanket of sensory seduction. Despite her anger at him, her lower belly clenched in intense anticipation.

Her heart hammered at a rampant pace, but she replied in an even tone, "I'm sorry, but I'm an animal doctor."

Ty's hands encircled her waist and his warm breath tickled her neck as he bent close to her ear. "I've got the right doctor, all right. I definitely feel animalistic whenever I'm anywhere near you, Doc."

Evan's stomach flip-flopped at his sexy comment. His heat had begun to permeate her white coat while tiny tingling waves of awareness spread from his hands clamped around her waist down to her belly and straight to her core. She closed her eyes against the sensations clamoring inside her.

"Why are you here?" She finally got the words out that had lodged in her throat.

Ty kissed her neck then nuzzled the soft skin. "Because every day without you was pure torture. You made my pulse race whenever I caught sight of you or inhaled your sweet scent. You made me look at who I was and learn to laugh at myself again… Evan, you're the vitality missing from my life. When I'm with you, I feel whole."

She held back a sob at his declaration, but she couldn't hold back the tremor in her voice. "Why didn't you call me?"

Ty turned her around. His green gaze searched hers as he clasped her shoulders. "Because I didn't want to be hurt again. But I realized that you're all I want, and if sharing you with your career is the only way I can be part of your life, then I'll have to come to terms with that."

Tears surfaced as she gripped his chambray shirt. "But you live in Maryland."

The tiny scar above Ty's right eyebrow added a sexy ruggedness to his good looks. His devastating smile made her heart skip several beats.

"Actually, I'm renting out the Double D for a few months."

Her stomach clenched at his words. "A few months?"

Ty nodded. "It takes a while to build your dream home if you want to do it right."

Evan swallowed the lump of heart-wrenching emotion that welled up in her throat. "Your dream home?"

Ty unbuttoned the two buttons that held her long white coat closed and slid his hands under her white linen shirt. Grasping the smooth skin at her waist, he pulled her close. "*Our* dream home with plenty of property for animals to run."

The serious intensity in his voice made her thighs begin to tremble. Did that mean what she thought it meant?

"That is if you'll consider sharing your life with a man who'll need to know from time to time he's still a high priority in your life."

Evan's blood rushed in her ears and her heart thumped at a rapid pace. "Sharing my life? Are you asking me to marry you?"

Ty's white teeth flashed. She loved seeing those crinkles around his eyes once more. "Do you think the sheriff would have it any other way? Though he probably would like our kids to have the 'Masters' last name, I'm a selfish bastard. I want to make sure you're mine 'til death do us part."

Evan was completely floored and beyond thrilled by Ty's marriage proposal.

She wrapped her arms around his neck and kissed his jaw. "You think you can handle me?"

Ty chuckled. "No. I'll probably spend the rest of my life trying though." His gaze turned serious as he finished, "But I'll die a happy man, nonetheless. Will you marry me, Evan?"

Evan narrowed her gaze. "I think you've got a lot of gumption showing up and asking me to marry you after leaving me like you did."

Sincere guilt settled on Ty's features. "I'm truly sorry if I hurt you by not returning your call. But I knew if I called you, I'd want to see you and the cycle would start all over again. I had to come to terms with myself first. Do you understand that?"

Evan shook her head. "Nope. I'm not the kind of person who just sits and waits for others to come around."

Ty raised his dark eyebrows. His hands tightened around her waist. "What are you saying?"

She moved her nose close to his neck and inhaled. Ty's spicy scent intoxicated her like no other. The man truly had her dangling on a string. She pressed her lips against his jaw, enjoying the rough texture of his five o'clock shadow scraping her mouth.

She met his gaze with a steady one. "I have a plane to catch in less than two hours."

Ty's jaw ticced as he set her away from him. His hands slid down to grip her hips in a firm hold. Deep hurt reflected in his dark green eyes. "Who is he?"

Tears shimmered in her eyes, blurring her vision as deep emotion gathered up within her. "I planned to go after the man who taught me to grow up both physically and mentally in a very astute and loving way. I wasn't about to let him slip through my fingers. If he didn't have faith, I had enough belief for the both of us."

Surprise crossed his features. "You were coming to Maryland?"

Her quick nod caused unshed tears to roll down her cheeks. "I didn't know what I was going to say to you. But I figured the words would come when I saw you again."

Ty cupped her jaw and rubbed his thumbs along her cheeks, wiping away her tears. His deep green gaze sought the truth. "Do you love me?"

She put her hands over his and nodded. "So much it hurts."

Ty pulled her to his chest and wrapped his arms around her in a tight hold. He kissed her hair and gave a half-laugh. "I'm glad to know I'm in good company."

Reaching for her hand, he tugged her behind him as he made his way out of the exam room. "Come on, Doc. There's something I've been dying to show you."

Evan's hand tightened around Ty's to slow him down so she could grab her purse from behind the counter. She released his hand long enough to remove her coat and hang it on a hook behind the door. Once she retrieved her keys and locked her office door, she allowed him to escort her to his car.

As Ty opened the passenger door, Evan smiled at the shiny black Mustang with its convertible top folded down. "Nice car.

I'm glad it's a warm day. Did you do a long-term rental for this one?"

Ty shut the door behind her once she'd settled in the seat. "No, this one's bought and paid for."

Her surprised gaze followed him until he settled in his seat and started the engine. "When did you buy it?"

"Last week." Ty put the car in gear and backed out of the parking lot.

Last week? She frowned and her stomach tensed. "How long have you known you were coming back?"

"Two and a half weeks."

Evan's heart rate elevated in time with her temper.

"Ow!" Ty jerked his gaze to hers when she punched his arm. "What was that for?"

"For putting me through hell for so long when you knew you were coming back."

Ty rubbed his biceps and met her gaze before returning his line of sight to the road. "I had to talk my partner into working with me on a long-distance basis, buy land, buy a car, talk to Jena about renting out the Double D property, take care of clients at work—"

"There's one thing you forgot to do in all your planning," she interrupted him. "Tell me that you love me and find out if I felt the same."

His gaze snapped to hers and desire burned in the green depths. Grasping her hand, he kissed her knuckles. "I loved you from the moment you threw a towel over my head, tied me up and threatened to stick it to me, Doctor Masters. As for you loving me..." He glanced at the road then winked at her. "If I had to, I planned to wear you down until you admitted you loved me just as much."

Happiness radiated through her when she finally heard him say those three little words and that he wouldn't have given up on them. Leaning back in the leather seat, she put her booted foot on the console between them and pulled her skirt higher, exposing her knee.

"So tell me what you've been dying to show me."

Ty took his gaze off the road for a second, saw her exposed knee and jerked his gaze back to hers. His lips tilted in a sexy smile at the same time his hand landed on her knee.

Evan returned his smile and pulled the clip out of her hair, tossing it in the backseat. Running her fingers through her hair, she enjoyed the sensation of the hot Texas wind whipping at her locks.

When Ty's hand slid to her naked thigh and he began to massage the firm muscles, Evan's body ignited. Pulsing heat flooded her lower body while her heart rate revved to the point she had to hold back her pants of anticipation.

Ty kept his eyes on the road as he massaged her leg in attentive, seductive circles while slowly moving his hand lower with each rotation.

Evan saw the intent in the brief hooded gaze he cast her way. He planned to draw this out, to make her wait and wait and wait before she exploded. But she had other ideas. She wanted Ty to totally lose it today—she wanted to finally see that primitive side to him she knew existed just below the surface.

Putting her hand over his, she moved his hand back to her knee. "Where are you taking me?"

Ty turned a raised eyebrow her way when she'd stopped his hand's descent, but kept his hand where she put it. "Back to our place."

"Ah." Evan trailed her fingers over his then slid her fingers down her thigh in a slow, seductive caress.

She watched Ty's reaction out of the corner of her eye. His gaze darted between the road and her leg so often she realized she was getting just as much attention as the road.

Evan slipped her hand under her skirt and ran one finger along her thong until she reached her center. Her underwear was already damp. Damn the man for making her want him so much.

"Why are we going back to the Double D?" She tried to sound casual as she slid her finger inside her body, but the knowledge Ty knew what she was doing, even though her skirt blocked his view, made her voice tremble in excitement.

"You'll see." Ty's gaze locked on her skirt-covered lap as she began to stroke in and out of her body. His hand on her knee tightened and a muscle jumped in his jaw.

"Come on, share with me." Her voice came out breathless and husky-sounding. She closed her eyes to try to focus. Her body was so primed she was beginning to lose her train of thought.

"Damn straight," Ty uttered as he grasped her wrist then slid his hand over hers. Before she knew what he intended, his finger joined her finger and he thrust them both deep inside her.

Evan's hips jerked at the sensual onslaught. Her eyes flew open and she locked gazes with Ty.

In response, he pulled their fingers out of her channel, wrapped his finger around hers then guided their entwined fingers back inside her. The added, twisted thickness, along with the slow and seductive, bone-melting intentional action made her heart stutter and her thighs tremble.

Ty returned his gaze back to the road as he stroked her body with her. Evan's breath came in short, choppy pants and her hips rocked of their own accord. She bit her lip as her entire body tensed.

"Come for me, sweetheart." Ty glanced at her as he slammed their hands against her, sending her right over the edge. She let out a low scream as waves of pleasure shot through her channel, spreading throughout her body.

When the last tremor stopped, Ty withdrew their hands from her body. Surprise filled her when he locked gazes with her for the brief second it took him to slide their entwined fingers inside his mouth.

While Ty let his line of sight return to the road, his warm tongue encircled their fingers, swiping her essence away. The action was so erotic and seductive all she could do was stare in entranced astonishment.

Ty's gaze remained straight ahead as his tongue darted between their fingers to capture every drop.

Evan's body began to react to the sexy stimuli. Her stomach tensed and her breasts swelled. She glanced at the road and tried to regain her composure.

Ty began to suck hard on her finger. The tantalizing pull made her nipples harden. She'd missed his attentive mouth.

He pulled her finger out of his mouth and laced his fingers with hers. Kissing her hand, he met her gaze. Hungry, lustful arousal reflected in his. "I've missed your sweet taste."

Ty left her totally speechless, yet once again, he'd turned their lovemaking around. Would she ever see his unrestrained side? Both satiated and frustrated, she bit her lip and stared at the trees lining the dirt driveway they'd turned down. She'd been so caught up, she didn't realize they were almost to the house.

Ty pulled up to the small ranch house and cut the engine. Without a word, he got out of the car and walked to her side.

Evan sighed as her gaze followed his confident stride. It didn't matter. The man made her shudder at his touch. He made her boneless putty in his hands. She couldn't expect to undo years of mental and emotional barriers overnight. But she had confidence she could break through one day.

Opening the door, he offered his hand to help her out of the car.

Evan took a steadying breath and put her hand in his.

Ty's grip on her hand felt tight. She had all of a second to glance up at him in surprise before he jerked on her hand and used the momentum to toss her over his shoulder.

"Ty!"

"Not one damn word!"

When he headed straight toward the barn, she smacked at his jeans-covered butt. "Hey! What gives?"

Ty closed the stable door behind him and set her booted feet on the hay-strewn ground. Regardless of his enigmatic behavior, Evan's heart rate shot up.

She barely had time to put her hands on his chest before he walked her back against the closed door.

Ty lowered his nose close to her neck and inhaled deeply as he pressed his chest against hers. "I wanted to take my time with you after being apart for so long." He pulled on his belt buckle and yanked at the fly on his jeans as his breath bellowed in and out in harsh gusts.

Evan's heart hammered at the barely held control emanating from him. Her hands lowered to his waist. "I want to see you let go," she whispered against his neck before she pushed his pants and underwear down his hips, jerking the material past his knees.

Ty's hands were already under her skirt pulling it up her thighs. His warm fingers slid along the back of her thighs where he gripped her muscles as he let out a harsh growl.

Evan moved her hands to his shoulders. Tight muscles flexed underneath the soft chambray material as if Ty were about to explode. She panted, her rampant breathing moving in tandem to the blood whooshing through her body.

Ty nipped at the skin between her shoulder and her throat right before he grasped her buttocks and lifted her thighs around his waist.

Her heart jerked in frenzied excitement when he pressed his erection against her wet underwear.

"You make me forget everything but being inside you."

She kissed his stubbled jaw and chuckled. "Like the fact I still have on underwear?"

Ty gripped her rear and jerked his hips. The primal action shoved his cock deeper inside her despite the cotton barrier between them.

"Do you really think a thin piece of material will stop me, sweetheart?"

His husky words coupled with the knowledge the small barrier of her thong was the only thing standing between them sent her libido into full tilt arousal.

She knew she could easily shift to the left or right and give him the access he craved, but Ty's intemperate mood was indescribably erotic, his aggressive actions so heart-stoppingly raw and real, she wanted him to find his way through the physical barrier between them. She wanted him to take their relationship to the uninhibited level she knew always existed just below the surface.

She kissed his neck. "You're all I've ever wanted."

Ty's mouth slanted over hers in a fierce, possessive kiss as he rammed his cock deeper inside her.

Evan whimpered and rocked her hips. Her lower belly knotted in anticipation and tears spilled from the corners of her eyes, her emotions were so intense. She throbbed with the need to feel him letting go of his steely control, to feel him taking her as hard and as deep as he could.

Ty's hands cupped her rear so tight she was certain she'd have dual bruises in the shape of his fingers as a reminder of their reunion.

The wood behind her back felt both rough and raw, but she didn't care. Her entire body jolted and shuddered with each dominant thrust. This was the Ty she'd wanted to experience. He didn't hold back. Instead he let pure emotion and instincts drive him. She'd damn well make sure he never held back from her again.

Evan broke their kiss and wrapped her arms tight around Ty's neck. "Go for it, good-lookin'." She locked her boots together at the base of his back, then lightly bit at the tendon flexing on his throat.

Ty let out a sound she never thought she'd hear from him. The deep, rumbling roar both scared and thrilled her at the same time he ripped right through the fabric separating them.

The sensation of his cock shoving deep inside her sent Evan's physical response straight through the roof. She screamed as her orgasm rolled through her in rapid pulsating waves of heart-pounding pleasure.

Ty's knees buckled for a brief second before he caught himself. He continued pistoning, rocking her against the door as he grunted through his own climax.

His head rested on her shoulder and with each upward thrust he groaned and clutched her closer. Through the last few lingering tremors of her climax, he didn't withdraw at all…he just let gravity take him as deep inside her as he could go. Evan didn't think Ty had ever been so physically and emotionally connected to her as he was at that moment.

Her emotions were riding so high and her heart beat so hard she had to take deep breaths to keep from feeling lightheaded. When Ty stopped moving and the only sound that filled the air was their heavy breathing, she panted out, "Yes, I'll marry you."

Ty pressed his lips to her throat then met her gaze. Even in the dim light filtering in the stables, she could tell deep emotions churned in his gaze.

"Good. I might've taken 'no' for an answer in the past, but this time around I refuse to accept anything but a 'yes'."

She tensed and raised her eyebrow, not liking the comparison between Lily and her. "Why?"

Ty pulled her away from the door and held her close. "Because I finally found a woman worth fighting for. I've never felt about anyone the way I feel about you. Plain and simple, you've stolen my heart and captured my soul. I love you, Evan."

Evan didn't think Ty could top the emotions he'd just aroused in her, but his words made her heart melt. "I love you, too."

When Ty withdrew from her and set her on the ground, she wrapped her arms around his waist and buried her nose next to his neck, hugging him tight.

A tiny, whimpering sound made her tense. The stables were currently unoccupied. At least as far as she knew.

Evan pulled back and met Ty's gaze. "Did you hear that?"

As soon as she spoke, she heard a scratching sound and another whimper.

Ty chuckled and straightened his pants while Evan fixed her skirt. "You had me so caught up, I forgot about the thing I wanted to show you."

He draped an arm around her shoulders and led her to one of the back stalls.

When Evan's gaze landed on the adorable black Labrador puppy staring at her through the plastic kennel's metal gate, her hands flew to her cheeks. Her lips trembled and her heart felt as if it were going to burst from her chest. She loved this man's thoughtfulness so much. "Awwww, he's just adorable!"

Ty walked into the stable ahead of her and unlatched the gate.

The puppy bounded out and jumped right into Ty's arms.

He turned to Evan and put the puppy in her outstretched hands. "She has a present for you."

Evan gave him a wary look as the puppy licked her cheek and nibbled at her chin. "When someone says, 'a puppy has a present for you', that usually isn't a *good* thing."

Ty didn't say a word. He just smiled.

Evan glanced back down at the ball of squirming fur in her hands. She lifted the pup to rub noses with her and that's when she noticed the dog's red collar had a ring attached to it.

She gasped at the sight of the diamond-covered silver band.

Ty's Temptation

Ty reached over and removed the puppy's collar. He slid the ring off the puppy's collar and held it out to her.

"I figured a doctor who probably takes gloves on and off her hands several times a day wouldn't have much use for a ring that sat up high, so I thought maybe channel set diamonds would do for an engagement ring. We can get it sized if it's too big."

Tears formed in her eyes once more. Evan's heart felt so full of love for this wonderful, thoughtful man. She cuddled the puppy under her right arm and held out her left hand for Ty to slide the ring on her finger.

The diamonds glittered even in the low light. Evan held up her hand and grinned at him. "You sure were prepared for a man who didn't know if I would say 'yes'."

Ty gave her a sheepish smile as he scratched the puppy behind the ear. "Well, I kind of had a feeling…"

Evan eyed him with suspicion. "What feeling?"

"When I saw you'd placed an ad for an assistant."

Disbelief rolled through her. She had no idea Ty was so impulsive. "You based life-changing decisions on the fact I hired an assistant?"

Ty shook his head and gave her a knowing smile. "No, Doc. I loved you and wanted to help you as best I could."

"How'd you help me?"

Ty replaced the puppy's collar around her neck and rubbed her muzzle. "How do you think I was able to convince my business partner that a long-distance partnership with me making a few visits to Maryland every month would work?"

Evan shook her head. "I don't know. How did you?"

His broad smile swept her away.

"That's because I told him I'd keep an eye on his baby sister. After all, I was the one who told her about a great job opportunity that had just opened up in Texas."

Evan's body tensed. "What's your partner's name?"

"Peter Shannon."

Her eyes grew wide in shock. "Nicole is your partner's sister?"

Ty laughed. "Yep. I remembered that Peter had told me Nicole only had one more year to go to finish vet school, but she was having so much anxiety about her career path once she graduated the following year, that she planned to take a break for a year. So I told her about your job opening and said you were a wonderful lady who had a lot of knowledge to share."

Realization dawned and she narrowed her gaze. "Did you put her up to insisting on calling me Doctor Masters?"

Ty chuckled and raised his hands in an innocent stance. "Nope. Not guilty." Then he grinned. "But I knew I loved Nicole for a reason."

He cupped her cheek and his expression turned serious. "I would never have given you a pet if I didn't think you wouldn't have time to spend with it, Evan."

Evan was speechless. She'd never felt such deep feelings for another person. Her tears fell onto the puppy's soft coat as she rubbed her cheek against her neck.

"What are you going to name her?" he asked in a quiet voice.

Evan glanced down at the dog chewing on her shirt and kissed the top of her head. Intense emotion welled up inside her as she met Ty's steady gaze. The man had given her so much—love, a future and a companion for life…of both the human and the animal variety.

"I'll call her Shadow because she's going to be mine at home and at work. I think my office needs a mascot, don't you?"

Ty wrapped his arms around Evan and the puppy. Holding them close, he kissed Evan on the temple then inhaled next to her neck as if he couldn't get enough of her. "I think that's a great idea, Doc."

Epilogue

"That was a wonderful dinner, Evan. I had no idea you could cook like that." Harm set his napkin on the table and leaned back in his chair with a grin on his face.

"I agree, girl. You're an amazing cook." Jena stood and collected Harm's and her plates from the table. She glanced at Harm and continued, "It's a good thing Harm can barbeque with the best of them, because I'm helpless in the kitchen."

Ty wrapped his arm around Evan's waist as she picked up his plate along with hers. Pulling her close, he winked at his wife. "Told you she made killer Chicken Marsala. Yep, she's a keeper all right."

"You'll just have to work out twice as hard, or we'll have to roll you out of this house when it comes time for you to move to your new home." Harm cut his amused gaze to Ty.

"Speaking of which…" Ty pushed back his chair and came around the table, nodding to Harm. "Come on. Let's get a beer from the cooler outside. Then I'll show you my blueprints for the house."

"That the beer left over from Jake's picnic?" Harm asked as he stood up.

"Yep, I didn't bother bringing it inside since I knew you two were coming over tonight."

"Ahem, thanks for the help," Jena said when her husband started to walk away with Ty.

The two men slowly turned and met each other's gazes for all of two seconds before they both said in unison, "Do you want us to help clean up?"

Evan set the dishes on the counter and waved them away with a dismissive gesture.

"Go on with yourselves. You'd be more a hindrance than help in this tiny space Aunt Sally called a kitchen."

After Ty and Harm walked outside, slamming the screen door behind them, Jena chuckled. "I've never seen two men move so fast, have you?"

Evan snorted as she turned on the warm water to rinse the dishes. "They wanted to make sure they were out of 'calling' range in case we changed our minds."

Jena tucked a strand of her blonde hair behind her ear then started to gather up all the utensils from the table. She paused and her gaze locked with Evan's, mischief dancing in her blue eyes. "Couldn't you just see the wheels turning in their heads as they stared at each other? You know their thought processes were as basic as 'Am I going to look like a pansy-ass in front of my brother-in-law if I cave?' Which quickly switched to 'But damn it, I don't want to fuck up tonight and end up having to fall asleep with a hard on'."

Both women burst out laughing.

"How much longer on your house?" Jena asked as she took over rinsing the dishes.

Evan took the rinsed plate Jena handed her and opened the dishwasher. "According to Ty, our house should be finished in three months." She set the plate in the dishwasher then glanced around the small house. "I'm going to miss this place. It's small and cozy…"

"Go get it, Shadow!" Ty's voice carried through the screened door.

Evan paused and smiled. Ty must be throwing the ball for their puppy. "I swear Shadow would chase that tennis ball all night as long as Ty continued to throw it for her. But she's getting too big to run around in this tiny house."

"Well, at least you won't be too far away from us. I was glad Ty bought the Timmon's land. Those eight acres will be plenty of room for Shadow to run.

Once she'd filled the dishwasher, Evan turned it on and then wiped down the table. Handing the cloth to Jena, Evan leaned back against the counter as Jena finished washing the last two pans in the sink.

"Have you noticed our men have been out there for fifteen minutes? It doesn't take that long to find a beer in a cooler full of ice." Evan folded her arms and gave a rueful smile.

Jena laughed. "That's because they wanted to make sure they were out there long enough so we couldn't assign them any additional after-dinner chores—hence the 'let's throw the ball for the dog ruse'." When she finished speaking, she gazed out the window as if she were looking on the porch for their absentee spouses.

Then Jena turned to Evan. "I know…well, I know you were a virgin before you met my brother and if you have anything you want to ask, feel free." A wicked smile tilted the corners of her lips. "How about a tip to jazz things up a bit?"

Jena's comment piqued Evan's curiosity. Evan turned and leaned her hip on the counter. "I'm all ears."

Jena's gaze darted to the closed screen door. "Have you ever tried Altoids?" she asked in a low voice when her gaze returned to Evan's.

"I'm assuming you mean for more than fresh breath and that this is something Ty would really like?" Evan smiled and reached for her purse that had been leaning against the backsplash on the counter.

Jena rubbed soapsuds over the dirty pan and her grin turned sly as she nodded. "It'll keep things spicy, that's for sure."

Evan pulled out a tube of lip gloss from her purse and spread a thin layer over her lips as she spoke, "Hmmm, no. Can't say I've ever tried that one." She put her lip gloss away in her purse and winked at Jena. "Thanks for the tip. I'll have to give that one a whirl."

Jena chuckled. "Just don't tell my brother the tip came from me. The knowledge might short-circuit his brain."

"Mum's the word." At the sound of men's boots walking on the wooden planks outside, Evan cast her gaze back toward the open door. She quickly slid down the counter until she was shoulder to shoulder with Jena. "I found this really cool lip gloss. It's…well, it's hard to explain."

Jena stared at Evan's lips in puzzlement. "It just looks like clear gloss to me. No color."

Evan shook her head, feeling the devil on her shoulder as well as the herbs in the lip gloss doing their work. But she thought a person as free-spirited as Jena would appreciate the benefits. "No, that's not what I meant. We were talking about tips."

Jena's eyes widened in understanding and she leaned a little closer. "Tell me before the guys come back in."

Evan grinned. "Nah, I think I have to show you." Before Jena could move, Evan cupped her sister-in-law's cheeks and planted a solid kiss on the other woman's lips.

"*That's* not something you see every day," Harm's deep voice sounded across the room.

Evan pulled away from Jena, dropping her hands. Her cheeks turned hot in embarrassment. She hadn't meant for the guys to see that. She glanced back at her husband and Harm standing there holding beers. Interested surprise lit their faces.

When Evan returned her gaze to her sister-in-law, Jena had a shocked, wide-eyed look on her face. The other woman's gaze darted to her husband and then her brother as she pulled her lips inward.

Evan's heart pounded. God, had she totally wigged Jena out? She wasn't coming on to her. She'd only wanted to show her…

Jena began to rub her lips together back and forth at the same time realization dawned on her expression. "What'd you say the name of that lip gloss was?"

Obviously Jena's lips had started to feel hot and tingle all over. Evan let out an inward sigh of relief. She laughed and pulled the tube out of her purse to show Jena. "It's called Kiss Me, Baby."

"Do you have any idea what the hell is going on?" Harm asked Ty.

Evan glanced at her husband to see him shrug his shoulders. "Beats the hell out of me. I just wish the other woman in this scenario wasn't my sister. I feel cheated somehow."

Evan rolled her eyes at Ty and turned back to see Jena quickly rinse the last pan, set it to the side and dry her hands. "What's in it?" She reached out and took the tube of lip gloss from Evan's hand.

"It's supposed to be one of those lip plumper products," Evan explained as Jena examined the ingredients with interest.

"Ah, now I see." Ty's comment had Evan glancing his way. The dark, sexy look her husband gave her took her breath away. Ty winked at her as he clapped Harm on the shoulder and continued with a chuckle, "Come on, I'll show you those blueprints."

"We're stopping by the store on the way home," Jena called out to Harm.

Ty groaned at her comment. "I *really* didn't need to know that."

Evan couldn't help but laugh at Harm's 'you're all nuts' expression. "Just stop by the store, Harm. Trust me."

"Think Altoids," Jena prompted her husband.

"Altoids?" Ty asked, raising his dark eyebrows.

A wicked grin spread across Harm's face as if he enjoyed being the one in the know this time. "Stop by the store, Ty. Trust me. It's worth the trip."

Enjoy An Excerpt From

COLT'S CHOICE

Copyright © PATRICE MICHELLE, 2004.

All Rights Reserved, Ellora's Cave, Inc.

∞

Rockin' Joe's was just as he remembered it, a good-time bar with lots of drinking and dancing. As he walked through the dim, smoke-filled room, country music playing in the background, he spotted Mace and Elise sitting in a secluded corner booth. He'd bet his last dollar Mace had brought many dates to that very booth. Colt set his teeth and headed for the table, his boot heels making a dull thud on the wood floor as he walked.

When he slid into the bench seat beside Elise, she was now sandwiched between both Tanner brothers. Just as he'd settled in his seat, Mace grabbed Elise's hand as *All My Exs Live in Texas* started up in the background.

"Come on, Elise, they're playin' our song," he drawled as he pulled her out of the other side of the booth.

"See you in a few, Colt." Elise turned and smiled back at him as Mace led her to the dance floor.

Colt watched his brother swing Elise in his arms. His chest tightened as she laughed up into Mace's face when she missed a step and tripped. Mace caught her and pulled her closer. Colt fisted his hands beneath the table and set his jaw. He wanted to punch Mace's square into the middle of next week.

Thankfully the song ended and Mace escorted a breathless, rosy-cheeked Elise back to the table.

She fanned herself and smiled. "Can you get me something to drink, Mace? It's hot in here."

Mace slid back out of the booth. "Anything in particular?"

"How about Sex on the Beach?" She grinned at him and gave Colt a sideways look. "I haven't had that in a while."

Colt groaned inwardly. The woman was way too sassy for her own good.

Mace gave him a suggestive smirk before he swaggered away. Colt turned his gaze to Elise and chose a neutral subject. "Looks like you had a good time out there."

Her sparkling green eyes met his. "Yes, I did. I've never danced the two-step before. It was fun to learn."

"How's the website going?"

"Great." Her face became more animated as she talked. "It's been a while for me, so I had to pull out my textbooks. The code was a little trickier than I had initially thought." She noticed his raised eyebrow and rushed to assure him, "But I think I have it all figured out."

Colt looked at her sincere face. "Something about you tells me you wouldn't let it go until you got it right, Elise."

As she gave him an appreciative smile, Mace returned with a whisky for himself, Sex on the Beach, complete with a cherry on top, for Elise, and a beer for Colt.

"Thought you could use one, bro," Mace said as he handed Colt a longneck.

"Thanks."

"Don't mention it."

As soon as Mace sat down, a redhead slid into the booth beside him, her arm going around his shoulders.

Her arrival made Mace scoot over and Elise in turn was forced to move closer, pressing her thigh against Colt's. A jolt of electricity shot through him as the heat of her leg touched his. With blood rushing straight to his erection, he had to focus to concentrate on what the redhead was saying to Mace.

"Where have you been, darlin'?" she drawled as she cut her eyes over to Elise, sizing her up.

Mace laughed and said, "It's good to see you, too, Lana," before he turned and introduced her to Elise and Colt.

Lana turned pouty lips to Mace as a slow song started to play. "Come dance with me, Mace honey."

Mace glanced at Elise as if asking for permission.

She laughed and shooed him on. "How could you possibly turn her down?"

As Mace slid back out of the booth, this time to be led away by the lady, Colt and Elise watched the well-endowed redhead wrap her arms around Mace and pull him flush against her body.

After a few minutes, Elise must have realized she was still pressed against him because she breathed out an embarrassed, "Oh," and moved over a few inches in the booth.

Colt wanted to tell her to stay but knew better. He didn't say anything even though he missed her soft heat already.

They drank their drinks in silence. He felt her inquisitive gaze on him as if she were probing him and wondering about his thoughts.

He refused to look at her. He didn't want to look down into those gorgeous emerald eyes, the kind of eyes a man could lose himself in if he wasn't careful.

Mace and Lana came back to the table laughing, arms wrapped around each other. They sat back down, on the other side of Elise, forcing her to move back over against him once more.

Colt swallowed hard. He didn't know how much more he could take. He and Elise listened as Mace and Lana exchanged all kinds of sex innuendos. His own libido had kicked into overdrive with the first brush against Elise, he didn't need any more stimulation. He felt like yelling, "Will you two get a room, already?"

He chanced a glance at Elise. Big mistake. She had finished her drink and proceeded to suck the last of the drink out of the cherry. She met his gaze and popped the whole cherry, stem and all, past her luscious lips into her mouth.

He went rock-hard instantly but resisted the urge to growl out his sexual frustration.

Lana slid out of the booth and said to Mace, "Come on, sexy."

"Sorry, Lana, but I brought Elise tonight."

Lana frowned and Elise cut in, "It's okay, Mace, Colt can take me home."

And straight to bed, Colt thought without really thinking. He was thinking with one part of his body, that's for damn sure. He wanted her so bad his balls throbbed. Why was wanting her such a bad idea again? he argued with himself as the seductive pull Elise seemed to have over him reached out, grabbed hold of his gut and squeezed. Tight.

When Lana licked her ruby red lips in a suggestive manner, Mace turned to Elise and Colt, saying as Lana pulled him away, "I love it when a woman knows how to use her tongue for more than just talkin'." He saluted them both as he walked in the direction of the exit with Lana.

Colt looked back at Elise, his body literally aching. Aw hell, he could keep his emotions out of the mix. The truth was, physically he'd never wanted a woman as much as he wanted this one. One way or the other, he'd convince her to make their unplanned date tonight a real one.

"Don't worry, Colt. I'll get a cab. I just didn't want Mace to worry about having to take me home."

When she finished speaking, she smiled at him. With a secret look in her eyes, she touched her lips, then put something in front of him on the table. "Night, Cowboy," she said in a sexy Virginian accent as she started to slide out of the booth.

Colt looked down at the table in front of him. Sitting on the table was the cherry stem tied in a nice, tight knot. And damn, she had done it all with that delectable tongue of hers.

"Not so fast, Princess." He put a staying hand on her thigh.

Why an electronic book?

We live in the Information Age—an exciting time in the history of human civilization, in which technology rules supreme and continues to progress in leaps and bounds every minute of every day. For a multitude of reasons, more and more avid literary fans are opting to purchase e-books instead of paper books. The question from those not yet initiated into the world of electronic reading is simply: *Why?*

1. ***Price.*** An electronic title at Ellora's Cave Publishing and Cerridwen Press runs anywhere from 40% to 75% less than the cover price of the exact same title in paperback format. Why? Basic mathematics and cost. It is less expensive to publish an e-book (no paper and printing, no warehousing and shipping) than it is to publish a paperback, so the savings are passed along to the consumer.
2. ***Space.*** Running out of room in your house for your books? That is one worry you will never have with electronic books. For a low one-time cost, you can purchase a handheld device specifically designed for e-reading. Many e-readers have large, convenient screens for viewing. Better yet, hundreds of titles can be stored within your new library—on a single microchip. There are a variety of e-readers from different manufacturers. You can also read e-books on your PC or laptop computer. (Please note that Ellora's

Cave does not endorse any specific brands. You can check our websites at www.ellorascave.com or www.cerridwenpress.com for information we make available to new consumers.)

3. *Mobility.* Because your new e-library consists of only a microchip within a small, easily transportable e-reader, your entire cache of books can be taken with you wherever you go.

4. *Personal Viewing Preferences.* Are the words you are currently reading too small? Too large? Too... ANNOYING? Paperback books cannot be modified according to personal preferences, but e-books can.

5. *Instant Gratification.* Is it the middle of the night and all the bookstores near you are closed? Are you tired of waiting days, sometimes weeks, for bookstores to ship the novels you bought? Ellora's Cave Publishing sells instantaneous downloads twenty-four hours a day, seven days a week, every day of the year. Our webstore is never closed. Our e-book delivery system is 100% automated, meaning your order is filled as soon as you pay for it.

Those are a few of the top reasons why electronic books are replacing paperbacks for many avid readers.

As always, Ellora's Cave and Cerridwen Press welcome your questions and comments. We invite you to email us at Comments@ellorascave.com or write to us directly at Ellora's Cave Publishing Inc., 1056 Home Avenue, Akron, OH 44310-3502.

Discover for yourself why readers can't get enough of the multiple award-winning publisher
Ellora's Cave.
Whether you prefer e-books or paperbacks,
be sure to visit EC on the web at
www.ellorascave.com
for an erotic reading experience that will leave you breathless.